Praise for Eastern Shore Shorts

In Gail Priest's Eastern Shore Shorts, *nine intertwined stories weave a tale of family, friendship, and following your heart. Priest's world is at once compelling, charming, and full of the wisdom, warmth, and beauty that is the Eastern Shore. Come for a visit, lose yourself between the pages, and savor every moment.* –Kathleen Long, *USA Today* Bestselling Author

Just spent the past several hours bingeing on Eastern Shore Shorts, *and if there were more, I'd keep reading. Gail really captures the essence of the shore . . . She knows her stuff. Love her characters and how they navigate their lives and how they decide whether to stay or go . . . I want to know what happens next to these folks. Really couldn't put it down.* –Liane Hansen, National Public Radio Personality

A collection of stories that reflects the unique character of these Eastern Shore towns and the intricately woven relationships of the people who call these places home. –Rachel Simpkins, Ward Museum, Salisbury, MD

This collection of short stories is a joy to read. Each one is like a lovely quilt square, perfect on its own, but when joined together and seen as a larger whole, the pieces form a breathtaking work of art. As I followed the thread of characters, I felt more and more connected to the larger story. The sign of an excellent book is that it lingers in the mind for days, and I definitely feel as though I've enjoyed a particularly sweet vacation on the Eastern Shore, where I've made many friends whom I'll remember fondly for a long time. –Tawdra Kandle, Author of the Love in a Small Town Romances

I love the way the characters in these stories are connected and pop up in different ways—like real life here on the shore. –Jane Richstein, Sundial Books, Chincoteague, VA

Gail Priest's Eastern Shore Shorts *is a heart-warming, sometimes gut-wrenching collection of vignettes set between the brackish Chesapeake and salty Atlantic backdrops in her closely observed Bay Hundred culture . . . Every reader will identify with the dynamic way Priest weaves grandiose dreams with the simpler, powerful truths of small town life. In* Eastern Shore Shorts, *love can harbor cruelty; loneliness can be a path to romance; old souls can feel like old friends in a heartbeat's glance. The denizens of* Eastern Shore Shorts *are long on driving passions and thriving spirits.* –Robert Blake Whitehill, Author/Screenwriter, The Ben Blackshaw Series, www.robertblakewhitehill.com

Gail Priest's Eastern Shore Shorts *effortlessly weaves together narratives that not only realistically represent the glory and beauty of Delmarva's Eastern Shore, but also introduce the reader to a diverse array of believable characters connected through blood, friendship, passion, or loss who, through their own unique and compelling journeys, come to the same understanding that love really does conquer all. Superbly written and a joy to read.* –Michael Sprouse, On-Air Host, *The Arts & Entertainment Report*, WRDE NBC, and *Coastal A&E*, Delaware 105.9 FM

OTHER BOOKS BY GAIL PRIEST

Annie Crow Knoll: Sunrise
Annie Crow Knoll: Sunset
Annie Crow Knoll: Moonrise

Visit Gail's website: http://gailpriest.com
Facebook: www.facebook.com/AuthorGailPriest
Newsletter: Tiny.cc/nueatx

Eastern Shore Shorts

Stories set in Berlin, Cambridge, Chestertown, Chincoteague, Easton, Rock Hall, Salisbury, St. Michaels, and Tilghman Island

Gail Priest

Cat & Mouse Press
Lewes, DE 19958
www.catandmousepress.com

Published by Cat & Mouse Press
Lewes, DE, 19958
www.catandmousepress.com

ISBN: 978-0-9968052-8-5
Copyright © Gail Priest 2018

This is a work of fiction. Names, characters, businesses, places, events, and incidents are either the products of the author's imagination or used in a fictitious manner. Any resemblance to actual persons, living or dead, or actual events, business establishments, or locales is purely coincidental.

The recipes contained in this book are to be followed exactly as written. The publisher and author are not responsible for your specific health or allergy needs that may require medical supervision. The publisher and author are not responsible for any adverse reactions to or damages caused by the recipes contained in this book.

Copy editing by Joyce Mochrie
Map by Erick Sahler
Cover illustration by Erick Sahler
Cover illustration Copyright © 2017 Erick Sahler

First printing 2018
Printed in the United States of America

Cat & Mouse Press
Lewes, DE 19958
www.catandmousepress.com

For the organizations and individuals dedicated to protecting and advancing the restoration and protection of the Chesapeake Bay watershed.

When everything is moving and shifting, the only way to counteract chaos is stillness. When things feel extraordinary, strive for ordinary. When the surface is wavy, dive deeper for quieter waters.

–Kristin Armstrong

CONTENTS

Acknowledgments

I want to thank Nancy and Joe Sakaduski for approaching me with this project. I am touched by the faith they have in me and my writing.

I appreciate Nancy's tireless effort and patience. Her unwavering dedication has made *Eastern Shore Shorts* a reality.

Gary Whitehair, of Chestertown, has been tremendously supportive and patient with all my boating, watermen, and crabbing questions. He and Lorraine Whitehair have been involved in my journey since my first novel, *Annie Crow Knoll: Sunrise*. I'm grateful for their constant belief in me.

John Swain, shipwright of the *Sultana*, was kind enough to make sure that the boatbuilding descriptions were correct.

When I called the Division of Natural Resources in Centreville, MD and began asking questions about commercial fishing licenses, Marie Myers, the Service Center Manager, generously gave me the answers and lots of ideas for making that part of the collection realistic.

Thank you to my beta readers Melinda Bookwalter, Skip Bushby, Gary Collings, Stephanie Fowler, Tawdra Kandle, Cindy Myers, Jane Richstein, Mary Scherf, and Rachel Simpkins. Your feedback and suggestions made all the difference.

I want to thank my husband, Gary Collings. He is the first to read everything, and he always has intelligent insights and powerful suggestions.

What an honor it is to have a cover by Erick Sahler, whose artwork I've admired for years.

I am thrilled to bring my readers back to a place I love. Thank you for your continued support and enjoy *Eastern Shore Shorts*.

THE COTTAGE

S WEAT RUNS DOWN INTO my eyes as I chisel wood away from the new boat rudder. I pause to wipe my brow on my T-shirt sleeve. Ella Fitzgerald begins to sing "Misty" on the boatshed radio I have tuned to the jazz station.

"Hey, that's your song." I give my boxer, Misty, a rub between her ears before returning to work. Her undocked tail wags.

I sigh. Although I haven't seen Lindsey for ten years, this song always makes me think of her. We were both eighteen. I was, and continue to be, too much in love. I try to focus on pushing my chisel through the wood with my mallet.

Out of the corner of my eye, I notice the boatyard cat sashaying past my dog.

"Leave it," I tell Misty.

My boxer's eyebrows rise. Her charcoal eyes follow the cat's tail. I know she wants to give chase, and the gray tabby is goading her to do it.

These two animals have been buddies since the day the tiny kitten was discovered crying underneath a cabinet in the boatyard office. She was quickly adopted as the Chesapeake Bay Maritime Museum mascot with everyone chipping in for the vet bills and food. We named her Edna Sprit after our 1889 bugeye, the *Edna E. Lockwood*, and the bowsprit of a boat.

Now the cat circles back to make another pass by my dog. Misty looks at me with a pleading expression.

"Oh, go ahead."

The dog is off faster than green grass through a goose. Edna Sprit scampers up onto the dormant ship saw. Not the safest place to claim. Misty stands below, barking.

"Edna Sprit! Find someplace else to land."

The cat wanders onto a nearby worktable.

It's time to head out. As I clean up my tools, Misty's barking, in the otherwise quiet shipyard, is getting on my nerves.

"Come here, girl."

Misty reluctantly abandons her job of watching the cat and pads over to me. I pat her head. Edna Sprit curls up to sleep.

The other shipwrights and apprentices left an hour ago. I stayed to figure out how to attach the hardware that will suspend the new rudder from the *Edna E. Lockwood*. Quarter-inch-deep grooves need to be roughed out of the three-hundred-pound rudder where the pintles will be attached. I began chiseling out the perimeter of one groove. It's a little tricky, but I'm making progress. I'll get back to it on Monday.

I turn off the radio. Before heading for my truck, I glance around at our progress on restoring the last working Chesapeake Bay bugeye. Bugeyes were log canoe sailboats used by watermen to access the shallow areas of the bay for dredging oysters. I fill with pride each time I realize I'm doing work that matters to the history of the Chesapeake. Other goals in my life may be lagging, but restoring historic boats has always been my dream. What I've helped to accomplish on the *Edna E. Lockwood* is most satisfying.

"Let's go."

Misty follows me out and jumps into the cab to ride shotgun, as usual. Before driving off the museum campus, I take my cell out of the glove compartment. My dad knows to call the office if I'm needed. Otherwise, I don't want the outside world disturbing me at the boatyard.

There is a text from Dad, but it's upbeat. He says that Mom is feeling better today, and they're going to the Friday night wine tasting at the Tilghman Island Country Store. I'm glad Mom has had a good day. I text back. "Have fun. I'll stop over tomorrow."

There's another text. I'm getting too popular for my own good. This one is from Parker, the kid I mentored a few years ago in the CBMM's Rising Tide After-School Boatbuilding Program. Parker just wanted to fish with his father, but he turned out to be a decent carpenter. He landed a basketball scholarship to college where he's just completed his junior year, but I know he'll become a waterman. Those roots run deep.

I read the text. Parker's still looking for summer work. His dad ran into some trouble and had to sell his workboat. I answer Parker. "Sorry. Still nothing at CBMM. Let's get together soon. And since you're legal now, I'll buy you a beer."

I turn over the engine and pull onto North Talbot Street but in the opposite direction from my apartment. I drive toward Tilghman Island where I grew up and where Lindsey and I spent our happiest times.

Lindsey was way out of my league, but for reasons I'll never understand, she fell for me. We met at the country club where I worked and her parents were members. They owned a vacation home in St. Michaels, while I was a local. But what Lindsey and I had in those years was something unexplainable. We were lovers, but we were also best friends. We finished one another's sentences like old folks who'd been married forever. I wanted to marry her. I still do.

When I reach Knapps Narrows, the Tilghman Island Drawbridge is up for a waterman directing his deadrise workboat home after off-loading his day's catch. Once the traffic resumes, I see my parents' Forester parked at the Tilghman Island Country Store, along with several other vehicles.

Misty gives a low bark.

"No, we're not stopping to see your grandparents right now.

Besides, I'd need a shower and a change of clothes before joining the wine tasting."

She eyes their Subaru as I pass.

I pat her head. "We're going out to the cottage."

Misty settles back down on the seat.

"That a girl."

When we near Saint John's Chapel, Misty sniffs the air.

"You know, don't you? Good dog."

I recall the day Lindsey and I discovered the nearly overgrown dirt path near the chapel. The area had never been cleared for farming, and the forest was dense. It looked like no one had traveled down the lane in a long time. After driving about a hundred yards, it seemed we'd end up stuck with no way to turn around.

Lindsey's eyes widened. "Do you think you ought to back it out?"

"Don't you want to see what's out here?" I asked.

She grinned.

Like excited children on a treasure hunt, we kept going. Eventually, we found an isolated cottage and a lovely view of the Chesapeake Bay. Since no one was around, we got out and began exploring. The two-story house was maintained, so we assumed it was a part-time owner. When we peered through the living room window, the furniture was old and modest, but there was a stone fireplace.

"This place is screaming for Arts and Crafts furnishings," Lindsey said.

My father was a furniture maker, but I wondered how Lindsey was familiar with the Craftsman period. "I'm impressed."

"You forget that my mom's an interior designer, and Dad's study at home is all Craftsman pieces. He loves the hand-built stuff."

"I wonder who lives here."

"I wish we did." Lindsey's eyes glistened. "Wouldn't this be the perfect place to raise a family?"

I took her into my arms. "I love you, Lindsey."

"I love you, too."

Every time we snuck out to our cottage, we found no owners. We brought out picnics and went swimming off the sandy beach. We made so many plans, but things began to change our third summer together, the summer before college.

I was going to be attending the International Yacht Restoration School of Technology and Trades for their boat-building and restoration program and working on my bachelor's degree in Rhode Island. Lindsey had been accepted at MIT and Berkeley for business. My vote was for MIT, which would put us about an hour and a half apart. We could see each other every weekend.

One day while we were lying on a beach blanket in front of the cottage, Lindsey said without warning, "I'm not sure about a long-distance relationship."

"Where is this coming from?"

She didn't speak. She only squirmed around on the blanket.

"Lindsey, we've had a long-distance relationship. You've been in DC every school year, and I've been here. We made out fine and with you going to MIT. . . ."

"I'm not going to MIT."

I felt my throat go dry. "You're not?"

"My parents think Berkeley is better."

I didn't want to start a fight, so I avoided saying that her parents didn't want her in New England near me. "That's so far away, but like I said, we're used to being apart for months at a time. We can make it work for four years."

"I'm going to need my master's degree to do what I want."

"Okay." I tried to sound optimistic. "I'll be back in four years, hopefully working at the maritime museum or building boats nearby, and you'll return a couple of years later, ready to advise these wealthy people on how to make more money."

She scrunched up her nose like financial planning was something distasteful. "I have bigger fish to fry."

I leaned in to kiss her. She put her hands in my hair, and the kiss deepened. When we came up for air, I whispered in her ear, "You'll come back to St. Michaels eventually, and I'll be waiting."

Tears swam in Lindsey's eyes. "My parents are selling the St. Michaels house."

I bit my lip. Now I knew for sure. They wanted to get their daughter as far away from the Tilghman hick as they could. "Why?" I tried to keep my voice calm.

"They're moving to the West Coast."

Man, the lengths these people were going to blew my mind. "Oh."

"I'm not coming back, Evan."

Her declaration shot my confidence, and I began to feel desperate. "How do you know that? Do you have some crystal ball or something? Besides, I thought we were living here." I gestured to the cottage.

Lindsey sat up. "We don't own this. We'll never own it."

"But you said—"

"They were pipe dreams. Not reality."

"So you were lying all this time."

She looked hurt and grabbed my hands. "No. I guess I thought it was only part-time. We'd live in DC or Baltimore or Philly and have a place here for a vacation home."

My instinct told me to pull my hands away, but I couldn't resist her touch. "I can't live in those places. You've always known that."

She let go and shifted farther away. The few inches between

us felt like a gulf.

"Lindsey, don't give up on me. I love you."

Tears slipped down her cheeks. "I love you, too, but I don't see things working out. We're from two different worlds, and we're going in opposite directions."

"And our love isn't enough?"

She glanced at me and shook her head.

"Jesus," I whispered.

"But we have the rest of this summer," Lindsey added.

"Great." I grabbed a handful of sand and let it trickle through my fingers.

"Look, maybe you're right. Maybe we will find a way back to each other."

"Don't bullshit me."

"I'm serious. I just need time to figure things out, but maybe we can make a promise to meet down the road to see if we still love each other."

"You mean wait and see?"

"Sort of."

I thought about this for a moment. "I can wait."

"You should date. You may fall in love with someone else and get married."

I started to interrupt, but she shushed me.

"But if we are both still single in, say, ten years, we'll meet to talk things over."

I looked around at the water, the sky, and the cottage. "I want to meet here."

Lindsey seemed unsure, but she finally agreed. "Okay. We meet here ten years from today."

And that was how we left it, ten years ago next month.

Whenever I came home from Rhode Island for holidays, I'd drive out to the cottage. Once I returned home for good, I visited regularly until a couple of years ago. Once, I actually met the owners. They were an older couple who had money but no time for their vacation property. They had been busy with careers and raising kids. Then they were busy with grandchildren. I didn't tell them about my youthful trysts out here with the girl I loved, but it was nice to see they were taking care of the place, even if it was unused. What a waste, but their absence had made me feel like it was mine. Eventually, I went less and less often because it began to feel unhealthy. Tonight will be the first visit in a long time.

As I pass Saint John's Chapel, my heart rate speeds up. No promises of anything more than agreeing to meet in ten years had been made. However, I have fantasies of Lindsey and me falling back in love and living happily ever after. I dated casually, but I never felt that intense connection to anyone but her. In my daydreams, when we meet at the cottage, she runs into my arms. She tells me that she still loves me. We get married, raise a family, and grow old together.

I shake my head. I have to get control of myself. She may not come back. She may not even remember. She could be married. The thought of waiting alone at the cottage puts a knot in my stomach. Perhaps that is why I am driving out here weeks early. I can sort of scope out the place and put things into perspective.

The first thing I see is the word SOLD on top of a FOR SALE sign at the turn-off. When the hell did this go up for sale? Maybe the couple gave up or died. I notice that the path out to the cottage is a real driveway. The trees have been pruned to allow heavy equipment through. Is our little cottage going to be torn down? Will it even be standing when Lindsey and I are supposed to meet?

It's discouraging to see how many modest houses and old cottages on the Eastern Shore have been bought, only to be bulldozed and replaced with McMansions. There are even developments of townhouses where there once were farm fields that led right down to the rivers and creeks.

My jaw tightens. "So many people are barely keeping a roof over their heads and food on the table, but these one-percenters are building monstrosities they don't need. They probably aren't even full-time homes."

Misty sniffs in agreement.

"Luckily, Tilghman hasn't changed too much, but it's creeping closer, and there's no way to stop it, girl."

Misty peers up at me with her dark eyes. She appears as sad as I feel. When I reach the end of the drive, I see that the cottage still stands, but it's been neglected. I pull over and get out of my pickup.

"Stay, Misty." She plops down on the seat.

I wade through the weeds and debris that have accumulated on what once was the lawn. Several of the porch floorboards need to be replaced, so I step gingerly past the front door with its real estate agent lockbox to peer through a dirty window. The curtain is tattered enough that I can see the old living room furniture is unsalvageable. From what I can make out, the dining room furniture isn't much better. In order to explore around back, I propel my body over the railing instead of chancing the steps disintegrating under my weight.

I hear a bark from the truck.

"Come on, then."

Misty jumps through the open window and trots along with me.

I'm surprised to find the back door unlocked. A musty smell hits me as I enter the kitchen. Old linoleum covers the floor. Some of the cabinet doors are hanging loose, and one is missing. There's no refrigerator or stove. There's an enamel-topped table but only three chairs, and one of them is laying on the floor with a broken leg.

My dog smells in the corners.

"I know it's past time for dinner. Be patient. There's nothing here for you."

She follows me up the stairs. I get a glance at the three small bedrooms and bath when Misty begins to bark.

"What is it, girl?"

I am trespassing, but I know every cop on the local force. I doubt I'd have much of a problem, but to be on the safe side, I go downstairs and out the back door with Misty at my heels. When we round the side of the cottage, instead of a patrol car, I find a silver Mercedes parked next to my beat-up truck.

Misty barks again.

"Quiet." She sits next to me with her lips curled.

A young woman steps out of the car. I wonder how she can afford it. She's wearing practical, but what I can guess is expensive, casual clothing. Her long, auburn hair is pulled back in a clip.

"May I help you?" she asks as she crosses the distance between us.

"I was just looking around. Are you going to tear down the cottage?"

"It's not mine."

"What are you doing here?"

"My client bought it."

She's not any of the agents from the local realty company listed on the sign. "I don't know you."

"No. But the person I represent has bought the property. I'm here to make some arrangements."

Misty growls quietly.

The woman backs up a few steps.

"Down. Quiet." Misty goes down but keeps her eyes on the lady. "She won't hurt you."

"You're trespassing."

She's decided to play hardball, so I know it's time to turn on the Eastern Shore charm.

"I'm sorry. I was just reminiscing. My childhood sweetheart and I used to say we were going to buy this place and live here. I didn't even know it was for sale. I would have bought it myself."

She looks at my jeans and T-shirt, which have been through a day of boat building. "You couldn't afford it."

"Ouch."

"I apologize. That was rude of me."

"Yes, it was. I work hard, but it doesn't mean I don't make a good living."

"Of course."

She was right, though. I could kick myself for not asking if the old couple I had met years ago would sell it to me. Now, any waterfront property, even a shack, was way out of my means.

"So back to my original question. Is your client going to bulldoze this piece of history and put up one of those obnoxious mansions?"

"I'm not at liberty to say."

I realize I'm not getting anywhere with this city slicker. "I don't want to waste any more of your time. Come, Misty."

During my lunch break the next day, I pop over to the realty office.

"Hey, Evan." Mary Kay has been the receptionist for as long as I can remember. She writes something on a sticky note.

"Hey, Mary Kay. How are you?"

"No complaints. How's your mother doing?" She puts down her pen and gets a dog biscuit out of her drawer for Misty.

"She has good days and not so good."

"Tell your momma I was asking for her. I've been meaning to call her for that peaches and cream pie recipe of hers." She gives Misty a good scratching behind the ears while the biscuit is being devoured.

"That could be a family secret."

Mary Kay laughs, but it's my grandmother's recipe, and I know my mother isn't going to let just anyone have it.

"What can I do you for?" Mary Kay asks.

"I want to find out who bought the cottage down that drive near Saint John's Chapel and what they intend to do with it."

I've never seen Mary Kay look flustered. She runs that office like a military officer, but she seems unsure of what to say.

Finally, she asks, "Why are you so interested?"

"Just curious, Mary Kay. Who bought it?"

"We don't know, and that's the God's honest truth."

I had no reason to doubt her, but I ask, "Didn't someone come in here to sign the papers?"

"A young woman did, but she was representing the buyer. She wears expensive clothes and drives a Mercedes."

"I know the one."

Mary Kay's eyes widen. "I wonder if it's some celebrity. You know there's been a rumor that Johnny Depp's been seen on a yacht on the Miles River."

"Yeah. I heard about that, but I doubt it's him who's bought the cottage."

"I'm sorry I can't help you."

"Thanks. If you hear anything, will you give me a call?" I wander toward the door. Misty stands up.

"Sure thing."

"It's going to piss me off to see that cottage bulldozed."

"They aren't going to do that."

"What?" I stride back to her desk. Misty collapses back down on the floor.

"The buyer's representative told me a crew of workers is coming to rehab it. They're all staying at St. Michaels Inn for a month."

"Why didn't they hire local people?"

"Evan, you and I were both born and bred here. You know it takes twice as long to get anything done because it's either crabbing or hunting season."

"I meet my deadlines."

"You're the exception."

The old saying was that if an Eastern Shoreman said he'd be there in a day, it meant a week. If he said a week, it meant a month. If he said a month, it meant a year. But I refused to perpetuate that stereotype.

"But this doesn't make sense. Who would pay that kind of money and not build their dream home?"

"I don't know."

"Nobody is happy with a simple cottage anymore."

"Well, they're saving it."

"That's something at least."

When I return to work, I decide to put the whole thing out of my mind and focus on the *Edna E. Lockwood*. Why torture myself about a property that I'm never going to own now? But after a few weeks, I notice that I'm irritable at the boatyard. My buddies are starting to avoid me because I'm not myself. Damn, I just can't stand not knowing what's going on out at the cottage. So for my sanity and the sake of my accommodating colleagues, I break my vow and drive out to the property after work. I just hope I don't run into Mercedes again.

I'm relieved to see there's no sign of her or the crew doing the rehab. It's mind-blowing how much they've accomplished in such a short amount of time. The weeds are gone, and all the trash has been removed from the yard. The entire exterior has been painted pale green, offset by sharp-white trim. The completed landscaping is the final touch on a property that now looks like something out of *Coastal Living*.

"Come on, girl. Let's poke around."

Misty's tail wags as I inspect the front porch where the steps and flooring have been repaired and painted. Through the window of the new front door, I can see the old wooden floors have been refinished, and the walls are painted a clean off-white. Newly installed blinds block my snooping eyes from seeing in the other front windows.

"Let's go around back, Misty."

On the exterior wall, I notice pipes roughed in for a new outdoor shower.

Misty gives a gentle bark.

"I know, girl. There's nothing better than showering outdoors." I scratch her neck. "Perfect for getting all the sand and dirt off a certain dog I know, too."

There's a new screened porch being added to the back of the house, which faces the water. I peer in the back-door window and see a modern kitchen with tile flooring. The counters and backsplashes aren't in yet, but there are Craftsman-style cabinets and stainless-steel appliances. The new owner is sparing nothing.

Misty and I are walking toward my truck when Mercedes pulls up.

"Trespassing again?" she asks, but without malice.

"I was hoping to make a clean getaway this time."

She smiles. "Since you're so curious, why don't you come in to see it?"

"Your client won't mind?"

"It will be our secret."

"He must have a huge crew working on this. I can't get over how much has been accomplished."

"Come in and see what you think."

As we enter the cottage, I become distracted by how dirty Misty's feet must be.

"Stay on the porch, Misty." I pull off my work boots and leave them by the front door.

The living room stone fireplace is now flanked with built-in bookshelves. When I notice what looks like the clean lines of an antique Stickley Mission Style rocker and two chairs, I ask, "Are those the real thing?"

"Yes."

"Not new?"

"No."

"Wow." New Stickley furniture is out of this world, but the antiques cost mega-bucks. "This guy must be loaded with money."

Mercedes clears her throat. "We are trying for a masculine look, but something that a woman would also enjoy."

"Rustic as opposed to shabby chic?"

"Do you like shabby chic?"

"God, no."

She leads me through the empty dining room and into the kitchen. "We're thinking of granite for the countertops."

"Has your boss considered cement with chips of recycled glass in it? I've seen some with flecks of glass that would fit in with the beachy feel."

She nods. "Yes, that would keep it lighter in here."

"I like it better than the granite. Not that you were asking my opinion, were you?"

Mercedes turns to look me in the eyes. "Do you want to see the upstairs?"

As I follow her up, I realize that I don't know her name. I can't call her "Mercedes" out loud. "Sorry, I didn't catch your name."

She shakes my hand at the top of the steps. "I'm Cait."

"Hi, I'm Evan."

She opens a door. "We tore out the entire bathroom."

The new fixtures have clean lines, and where the old bathtub once sat is a tiled, walk-in shower.

"This is fabulous."

"We'll be getting the bedrooms done with Stickley as well. We found some original antiques, but mostly it will be the new stuff. It's so well done, it blends perfectly."

I like this guy's taste so much, I think about showing up with a six-pack and some ribs when he's moved in. But judging from his expensive taste, red wine and some filets might be better. I'd never had a filthy rich friend, but who knows.

"So what do you think?"

"It's perfect, but doesn't he want an office?"

Cait pulls her phone out and types into it. "That's brilliant. Since there are three bedrooms, one of them should be a den or office. Thanks!"

I'm a bit confused but say, "You're welcome."

"Well, I need to drive back to DC tonight." Cait puts her phone away and starts down the stairs.

"What does this guy do?"

"High up in Google."

"Really. How often will he be able to enjoy this place?"

Cait shoos me out the door and locks it.

I sit on the porch steps to put my boots back on.

"It was nice to meet you, Evan." She shakes my hand again.

Part of me wants to tell her that I'm hoping, after ten years, the love of my life shows up here next week, but she pulls away before I make a fool of myself. Misty and I climb into the cab. I look at the cottage that is starting a new life of its own. Whatever happens with Lindsey, we won't be starting over here. It makes me sad, but hopefully this guy isn't a jerk. At least he works for a company with some social values.

I sit on the front steps of the cottage at nine o'clock. Stupidly, Lindsey and I never specified a time to meet. Well, we were kids. Time has a completely different reference when you're eighteen. Now we're twenty-eight, and the days go by much faster, just as my grandmother always warns. She says that the older you get, the faster time goes. Not that it's stopped her. She's in her mid-eighties and just moved into a new house in Berlin, Maryland. I guess having been a MASH nurse in Korea proved she had enough courage for anything.

Misty wants attention, so I play catch with her on the lawn. When she's finally worn out, I lie in the hammock that's been strung up between two trees and spend the time reading a book. My dog sleeps on the grass below me. At noon, Misty barks as a bright-red Dodge Ram with tinted windows pulls up. It must be the new owner, and this isn't good timing. Aside from having to explain why I'm lounging in his hammock like it's mine, I can't have him here when Lindsey arrives.

I haul myself up with a sigh. Misty trots next to me as I approach the truck. The driver's window rolls down, but the sun is reflecting off the windshield.

"I thought you'd look happier to see me after ten years," a woman's voice says from inside the vehicle.

I put my hand up to block the glare, and a head of shoulder-length, chestnut-brown hair emerges from the truck. She looks up at me. I freeze.

"Well, can't we at least shake hands?" Lindsey asks.

"I'm sorry. I thought you were someone else."

"Do you have more than one woman meeting you on this anniversary?"

I pull myself together. "Lindsey. It's really you." I open my arms, and she dives into them.

We hold on to one another tightly for a long moment.

"It's good to see you, Evan."

Tired of being polite, Misty bumps up against Lindsey's leg and woofs.

"And who is this beautiful girl?" Lindsey kneels and kisses my dog's head.

The boxer's unclipped tail goes a mile a minute.

"This is Misty."

"Misty, as in our song?" She smiles up at me.

I feel my knees weaken. "Yeah."

"Aren't you the sweetest thing in the world?" The dog wiggles under Lindsey's caresses.

"She likes you." My dog knows the score, that's for sure.

Lindsey straightens up and goes around to open the passenger side door. "She's going to like me even more when she sees what I brought for a picnic lunch."

I follow and grab hold of the cooler handle. "Allow me." I make an inventory of her rings. Nothing on her left-hand ring finger.

Lindsey takes out a big blanket, and the three of us walk around the cottage to the lawn overlooking the water.

"As you can see, someone has bought this place. They just finished a total rehab of it but haven't moved in yet." I attempt to hide my bitterness.

Lindsey begins emptying the cooler. "Sandwiches from the Tilghman Island Country Store, and what I hear is the best potato salad on the whole Eastern Shore."

I pull out a split of champagne. "Wow!"

"There are champagne glasses in there somewhere."

We settle down on the blanket to enjoy our lunch. Misty behaves herself as long as I keep her supplied with tiny bits of my food. Sitting here with Lindsey, eating a champagne lunch, is surprising and unexpected. It's the last thing I had envisioned and surpasses my expectations. But what does it mean? I want to know where we're going with this, but Lindsey just chatters on about who she ran into at the Tilghman Island Country Store.

She lies back on the blanket, and I want to kiss her. She's acting like no time has passed. As if we're going out again and together again. But ten years with no word from her hangs in my mind. *What has she been doing? Where does she live?*

"Lindsey, what's going on?"

She turns to look at me. "What do you mean?"

"We haven't seen each other in years. I don't know anything about you."

"I apologize. I got caught up in the nostalgia. It's great to see you, Evan."

"It's good to see you, too, but you aren't answering my questions."

"Well, I work as a senior project manager in Mountain View, California." She waves her empty ring finger. "I'm single, in case you were wondering."

I feel my face turning red.

"My career is everything I'd hoped it would be, and it came together much sooner than expected. I develop products based on research, data, and industry trends for worldwide monetization."

My eyes begin to glaze over, but I try to follow what she's telling me.

She sits up. "Let's go look inside the cottage."

"I'm sorry if I looked distracted. I do want to hear about your job."

"Enough about me. I want to check out the cottage." Lindsey stands.

"We're trespassing as it is."

"What's happened to your sense of adventure, Evan?"

"Well, they do have some amazing stuff in there now. The owner's hired hand showed me around one day." I scramble up onto my feet. "Let's see if it's unlocked."

A key materializes out of nowhere. Lindsey looks at the expression on my face and laughs. God, I adore that laugh.

"Why do you have a key?" I had only one glass of champagne, but I can't seem to follow along.

"Evan. Cait is *my* 'hired hand.' I bought the property for *you.* Cait oversaw the rehab, and between what I could recall and what she wheedled out of you, hopefully the cottage now looks like your dream come true."

"You bought the cottage for me?" I just about collapse onto the blanket.

Lindsey takes my hand, puts the key into it, and curls my fingers around it. "An outdoor shower and screened porch like you talked about when we were kids. You loved Frank Lloyd Wright and Gustav Stickley and Robert Morris designs. What I hadn't anticipated was the recycled glass and cement kitchen countertops. You surprised me on that, but Cait managed the change perfectly."

"Wait, you're the guy who's high up at Google?" I think I can hear the blood coursing in my head.

"Yes. Except I'm not a guy."

"Cait works for you?"

"Uh-huh."

I look at Lindsey, then at the key, and then at the cottage. "I can't accept this. It's too much."

"Evan, when you let me go ten years ago, I realized that it must have been so difficult for you. But you put my dreams ahead of your own. You loved me enough to give me flight. Please let me make one of your dreams come true. You always loved this cottage, and now it's yours."

"You're not coming back?"

"I can't. I'm sorry. I don't know if I'll ever find someone as wonderful as you, but I would suffocate if I tried to live here." She hesitates. "You wouldn't come to the West Coast, would you?"

I shake my head. "I love you, but this is where I belong." I don't need to tell her that my mom is sick. I'd be staying put one way or the other.

"That's what I thought. I understand that you won't leave. I hope you can understand why I can't come back. Or at least forgive me."

I pull her into my arms. "There's nothing to forgive."

"Kiss me, Evan."

I don't need to be asked twice. The taste of her takes me back years, and I want to make time stand still.

"Mmm." She runs her fingers through my hair.

Misty lets out a howl, and we both begin to laugh. I love the feel of her giggling against my mouth.

"Don't worry, Misty, I'm not taking him away from you," she says. "Let's take this party inside where we can be more comfortable."

We gather up what's left of our picnic, and Misty follows us onto the screened porch. She sniffs around while Lindsey unlocks the door into the kitchen. The dog finds a water bowl and sloppily laps up a drink as only a boxer can.

"You've thought of everything." I follow Lindsey into the now finished kitchen. "Wow! It's amazing."

She puts the leftovers into the refrigerator. "I'm glad you approve."

"I am really overcome by this."

Misty plops contentedly into a large dog bed on the floor, and within seconds, she's dozing.

"Come on, I want to show you everything." Lindsey takes my hand and practically skips with excitement into the dining room.

A Mission Style chandelier hangs over a handsome oak Stickley dining room table and chairs. The chair seats are upholstered in brown leather. The sideboard and buffet match the clean Mission lines.

"This cottage always screamed for your favorite style of decorating." She dashes into the front room.

I don't want to leave the dining room but can't wait to see my living room. *My living room.* This is unbelievable. Can I really accept this much from her?

"What do you think?" Lindsey stands by the stone fireplace with built-in bookshelves on either side. "A perfect place for all your books, and a cozy leather couch for reading."

"Lindsey." My brain is incapable of saying anything more than her name.

"I kept the Craftsman theme with the sofa, the foot stool, the coffee table, and the end tables. This rocker and the chairs are antiques, Stickley originals."

"Is this lamp a Tiffany?" I can hardly breathe.

"The glass lamp shade is, but the base is a reproduction."

"I can't accept all this."

"Oh, yes, you can. And you will. It's too perfect not to take." She bounds up the stairs to the second floor. "Wait until you see the view from the master bedroom."

When I reach the top of the stairs, she stops me.

"No, wait. I want to save that for last. First, we'll check out the other two bedrooms." She leads me into the first room. "We made this one into an office like you told Cait. We found the oak desk and chair and bookshelves for in here. But that can all be changed, if you prefer something else."

"Are you kidding? It's perfect."

"The other bedroom is for guests."

Although the guest room is filled with Mission furniture and the bed is covered with a Robert Morris fabric design, she rushes me through it, past the bathroom, and into the master bedroom.

I don't know what to look at first, the furnishings, the beautiful water view, or Lindsey. She's beaming with pride, and I can't take my eyes off her.

"Don't you like it?" she asks with childlike innocence.

"You're so beautiful and generous. I love all of it."

"For years, we dreamed about this cottage and how we'd decorate it. I'm lucky your tastes didn't change."

"Not one bit. And that includes my taste in women. You are the one I want, but it seems I can't have."

Lindsey pulls down the bedspread to expose fresh, new sheets.

"Are you sure you want to do this?" I ask.

"I've been waiting ten years."

"Oh, God. That puts a lot of pressure on a guy."

She laughs. "You've been waiting, too."

"Yes, I have."

She is standing on the opposite side of the big oak bed. I know I'm going to pay emotionally for this once she's gone. She's made it perfectly clear that she's not staying, but there's no way I'm keeping my hands off her. I cross the distance.

The click of Misty's nails on the wood floor wakes me up. I take a long, satisfying stretch, realizing I had dozed off after making love several times during the afternoon. I reach for Lindsey, but she's gone. I sit up. Misty's chin rests on the mattress, and her soulful eyes examine me.

"Just a second, girl."

I throw on my clothes, kicking myself for falling asleep.

My dog wanders to the bedroom door. It's time for her to eat and go out, but she seems completely content in her new digs.

I shove my shoes on, hopping along with one finger in the left one in an effort to get my heel into it.

"Lindsey?" I call as I rush down the stairs with Misty in hot pursuit.

There's no answer. I didn't really expect one, but I'm always hopeful.

I find a note on the kitchen counter.

> *Dear Evan,*
>
> *I fed Misty. She's been out to do her business. I couldn't wake you up. You were sleeping so soundly, and I hate goodbyes. We had a really painful one ten years ago, and I didn't want a repeat performance.*
>
> *You need to see Jenn Williams in Easton next week to sign some papers. She'll advise you on everything like insurance, taxes, and stuff. God, the property taxes are so cheap here. You have no idea what they are in California. It's insane.*
>
> *Don't let yourself feel guilty about this gift for one instant. Google pays me a ridiculous amount of money, and it means so much to me to make you happy.*
>
> *So have a happy life, my dear. Let another woman into that life. There's room for two here, and you can always build an addition for the children's bedrooms and maybe a family room downstairs for all their toys and the chaos. You deserve all of that.*
>
> *You'll always be my first and strongest love.*
>
> *All my love,*
>
> *Lindsey*

I carry the note with me onto the screened porch. The sun dips close to the water as the day wanes. Misty plops next to my feet. I sit on the floor with her and rub her back.

"Are you and Lindsey it for me?" I ask, expecting an answer.

Without lifting her head, she rolls her big black eyes up at me.

"You're right. Maybe not. There might be a woman out there who would put up with you and me just to live in this perfect cottage on the water. It's time to move on, girl."

ANTIQUES

Y OU DID WHAT?"

The expression on Connie's father's face was worse than she expected.

"I invited Audrey McDougal over for early dinner before the bathtub races."

"Who?" The vein in his forehead that popped up when he was upset was beginning to pulse.

"You know, the woman who moved into the Jacksons' house."

"The widow?"

"Yes."

"But we don't even know her."

"That's the whole point. She's my new neighbor and doesn't know that many people in town. I thought it would be nice to make her feel welcome."

"But our dinner at your house? Before the bathtub races next week? Why didn't you just take her to tea? Do some ladies' thing with her." That vein was looking about to explode. "I won't know what to say to her."

"Dad, you talk to everyone."

"Not to single women."

Connie rolled her eyes. "You talk to women all day long."

"That's different. That's sales." He huffed and began straightening a row of pocket watches that were in perfect order. He had carefully organized the display an hour ago.

When he got like this, he reminded his daughter of a stubborn bulldog. He had just turned eighty-five and showed little sign of slowing down.

Connie began unpacking teacups she had bought at auction yesterday.

Her father looked at the pink, yellow, and blue flowers on the cups. "They aren't your mother's, are they?"

"Of course not! I love Mom's 'Summertime' china set." She unwrapped another cup and held it up. "I got these cups at the auction."

"Oh."

"Why are you so grumpy?"

"Because you've included this woman in our traditional pre-bathtub races dinner."

"Why does that bother you so much?"

"Because you have ulterior motives."

"I don't."

"Will the boys and their families be coming to dinner, too?"

"Now you know they are always too busy getting ready for the races."

Connie and her husband, Jack, had started participating in the Berlin tradition with their two teenage sons the first time the bathtub races were held. Now in their forties, Kevin and Kyle took great pride in competing against one another, with their wives and children a part of whatever theme they each created.

"With just you and Jack, and me and Audrey, it will seem like a double date."

"And what's wrong with that?"

He turned, waving an antique rug beater at her. "You see. That's what you had planned all along."

"Be careful with that." She cleared a teacup and saucer out of his range.

"I am not going to start dating at my age. I'm too old."

"You're not too old to have a nice lady friend."

"Do you think I couldn't do more?"

"Too much information, Dad." Connie stuck her hands over her ears and closed her eyes.

"Your mother was my one and only."

"I understand that, but it's been three years since she died. I've had a few conversations with Audrey. She's smart and loves history. She served in Korea like you."

"Really?"

"The Army Nurse Corps." Connie knew that would impress him.

"Was she in a MASH unit?"

"I don't know. You'll have to ask her."

"Why did she move to Berlin, Maryland?"

"You should ask her."

"You've obviously talked to the woman, so tell me what you know."

Dad seemed hooked, so Connie decided to reveal a little more about her new neighbor on Bay Street. "Her husband died eight years ago, and at first, she didn't want to leave her friends and neighbors. But lately, it's been too long of a drive from the Western Shore to see her family. They're spread on the Eastern Shore from Tilghman Island to Ocean City, Maryland. She liked Berlin and decided it was close enough without being right on top of her children's families."

"Sounds independent."

"I think you have a lot in common." Connie smirked to herself. Her father still lived on his own in the house she had grown up in on South Main Street.

"What did you tell her about me?"

"Not much, other than you're a grumpy old coot who can't get a date." Connie busied herself with new orders of the locally made soaps and lotions she sold along with early twentieth-century china and kitchenware in her booth near the entrance of Town Center Antiques. Her father sold antique tools, watches, cameras, and small rugs in the booth next to hers.

"What did you really tell her?"

Connie shrugged her shoulders. "A little about your service in the war. She was very interested."

"She was? Hmm."

Connie knew how to keep him interested. "One of her grandsons is a shipwright at the Chesapeake Bay Maritime Museum."

"Is he involved in the *Edna E. Lockwood* restoration?"

"Again, something to ask her."

"I'm not talking to her."

"She also loves to read."

"Probably romance stories." Her father's mouth turned down.

"I don't think so. She's only talked about serious books. The kind you like."

"Nevertheless, I'm not coming to dinner, Connie."

"But you always have dinner with us before the bathtub races."

"I'll meet you out front here before the races start."

"But I told Audrey you would be eating with us."

"She won't care one way or another."

"What am I supposed to say to her? That you were too chicken to talk to her during dinner?"

"Tell her I got sick."

"But well enough an hour later to watch your grandsons running down North Main in bathtubs? Father, you are coming to dinner, and that's all there is to it."

"Who do you think you're talking to, young lady?"

"At sixty-four, I'm way past 'young lady.' Besides, you need a little push."

"Stop trying to micro-manage my life. Does this woman have any idea that you're trying to play matchmaker?"

"I wouldn't assume that she does. I just asked if she'd like to come to dinner and go to the races with us, and said that you would be joining us, too."

"Well, the woman should know what you're up to. Otherwise, she's going to feel like a fool. I know I certainly will."

"Stop referring to her as 'the woman.' Her name is Audrey."

Connie's father headed for the door of the antique mall.

"What are you doing?" Connie asked.

"It's slow in here. You can hold down the fort."

"But it's our turn to cover the front register. I can't watch the stalls and ring people up." Connie could feel her voice getting higher.

"Look, ever since your mother died, you keep pushing me here and there. I'm sick of it. You've stuck your nose in where it doesn't belong, so I'm going to go straighten this out."

"Where are you going?"

"None of your business." The door slammed shut behind him.

Connie winced. She didn't mean to upset her father.

She ran to the door, opened it, and called, "Dad. Wait! I'm sorry."

When he didn't turn around, she felt heartsick. Her mother would not have been happy with how Connie had handled this situation. She was forever saying, "Don't upset your father."

Audrey first noticed his beautiful snowy head of hair. The man led with that head as he strode up the walk to her new home. He obviously had something on his mind, but she wasn't exactly sure who he was.

"Hello!" she called out when he reached her steps.

He seemed a little startled. "I didn't notice you on your porch."

"You looked deep in thought." Audrey put her book down and walked to the screen door.

The man stayed on the steps. "I have no intention of intruding on your morning."

"But you're not intruding."

"I'm Dan Keas. My daughter, Connie, lives next door."

Audrey opened the porch door. "I'm Audrey McDougle. Won't you come in?"

"No. Thank you." He held on to the railing, but he was too robust to need to steady himself. It appeared to Audrey that he was trying to keep himself put in one place.

"Connie and her husband are lovely neighbors. I feel much better about moving here since meeting them. They have been very welcoming. In fact, Connie has invited me to dinner before the bathtub races."

"Yes, well, that's what Berliners do." He adjusted his eyeglasses on his nose.

When he either smiled or grimaced—Audrey wasn't sure which—he revealed a slightly crooked front tooth she found endearing. "Well, Berlin *was* voted 'Coolest Small Town in America.'"

"Is that why you moved here?" he asked.

"It may have factored into it, and it's the antique capital of the Eastern Shore."

Dan stammered. "Well . . . , I don't know about that."

"It says so on the town Facebook page, and everything on the

Internet is true." Audrey couldn't stop herself from winking.

He scratched his head. "Well, that's true. Oh, not the part about the Internet, but our Facebook page does say . . . you like antiques?"

"I love them. Are you sure you won't sit on the porch? I think we'd both be more comfortable."

"I don't want to bother you."

"It's no bother."

The man finally stepped onto the porch. Audrey let the screen door shut.

"I just wanted to let you know what my daughter is up to."

"She's up to something?" Audrey was a little confused but intrigued. "I hope it's something thrilling. She seems the type."

"Well," Dan looked around the porch, "she's doing a little matchmaking."

"Really? You and me?"

"Yes, I'm afraid so."

"Isn't that thoughtful."

A stunned expression appeared on Dan's face. "You don't mind?"

"Not at all."

"Oh, well." He wandered to one of the chairs.

Audrey sat in her chair so that he would sit. "I suppose you might feel like your daughter is meddling in your private life."

He nodded. "Yes, I do."

"Adult children can be overconcerned."

"Are your children that way? Telling you what to do as if you somehow can't manage anymore?" He sniffed.

"Maybe it's payback after us telling them what to do and not to do their whole lives."

Dan thought for a moment. "I think it might be."

"But, it's well-intentioned."

"I guess so. But I wanted to warn you. I didn't think it was fair for you to come to dinner without knowing the setup."

"Thanks. I appreciate it, Dan. I have been duly warned."

"You're welcome."

"Please tell me more about these bathtub races."

"I guess you've never been to one."

"No, but I'd like to know what I'm getting myself into."

This was the first time Dan truly smiled. "Folks build mobile tubs out of rain barrels, wheelbarrows, old metal washtubs, whatever, but the tub has to hold a minimum of two gallons of water."

"What do you mean by mobile?"

"They have to be on wheels to race down North Main Street. Sometimes people convert bicycles, but the tubs are mounted onto something with wheels. There has to be at least one rider, who often steers. Only one person can push the tub. Lots of times, they're wearing costumes like bathrobes and shower caps, but some costumes get pretty wild and have nothing to do with taking a bath."

"How many people come out to watch?"

"I think we had about a thousand last year. Businesses advertise on the tubs. It's a great boost for the restaurants and bars, too."

"I'm glad I've moved to the coolest town in the country." Audrey stood up. Dan shifted to rise.

"Please, don't get up. I was just about to get a glass of iced tea. Would you join me?"

Dan hesitated.

"Sugar or not?"

Dan settled more deeply into the chair. "Without. Thanks."

"Okay."

Audrey went past the last of the boxes she still had to unpack and into the kitchen. After putting glasses filled with ice and the pitcher of tea on a tray, she decided to cut two pieces of her peaches and cream pie.

Dan was reading the back of the book she'd set aside when she came to the doorway. He opened the screen door between the house and porch. She put the tray down on a table.

"Pie!" He sounded a little like the boy he must have been.

"I hope you're not diabetic. Connie will have my butt in a sling." Audrey handed him a piece.

"No. It's just so early in the day." Dan eyed his piece of pie. "Peach!"

"And cream." Audrey took a bite of hers.

Dan dug in. "Mmm. This is so good that I could eat it for breakfast, lunch, and dinner."

"It is before noon, but there's no alcohol involved. I figure at our ages, we should enjoy treats at any time of day."

"I agree. I turned eighty-five in February."

"Congratulations. I'm eighty-four."

"Oh, I wasn't fishing around for your age. My mother taught me never to ask a woman's age or her weight."

Audrey giggled. "I'll be eighty-five in October, and I weighed one hundred and forty-nine pounds at my last checkup." She picked up a fork full of pie. "After this, I'm sure I'll be over one fifty, but they're only numbers."

Dan looked at her with a pleasant expression. Then he gestured to her book. "So, you like historical fiction?"

"Does that surprise you?"

"Oh, no! I just haven't run into many women who read much more than romance novels."

"You need to get out more."

"Maybe I do."

Audrey picked up her book. "I should be unpacking the rest of my belongings, but I started this one last night. Read until I fell asleep, and I had to pick it right back up this morning."

"I'm interrupting your reading."

"It will keep. I'll have something to look forward to this afternoon. Do you like to read, Dan?"

"I do. Especially historical accounts and biographies."

"Have you read *My Own Words*?" Audrey asked.

"Yes. And I just got *Notorious RBG: The Life and Times of Ruth Bader Ginsburg.* Isn't that the most kick-ass title?" He paused. "Oh, I apologize."

"No need. It is a kick-ass title."

Dan smiled. "I'd be happy to lend it to you when I finish it."

"I'd like to put up one of those neighborhood library boxes in front of this house. I have so many books that it would be good to lend them out."

"Little Free Library." Dan took his last bite of pie.

"Yes, that's it. I want to encourage the reading of 'real' books."

"What's one of your favorites that you'd like to put in your lending library?"

"Nelson Mandela's autobiography, *Long Walk to Freedom*."

"That's a great choice."

Connie saw Marian and Ellen, two repeat customers from Easton, scurry into the antiques mall. "How are you ladies doing today?" she greeted them.

"We have exciting news," said Marian. "My son is marrying Ellen's daughter."

"Congratulations."

Connie remembered that Ellen and Marian had been best friends since childhood. She wondered how practical it was to have their children marry. It sounded like a recipe for disaster to her.

As usual, Marian was the one talking. "We drove to Berlin expressly to find enough antique hankies for everyone invited to the bridal shower."

Although she was the mother of the bride, Ellen just nodded.

After Connie quickly scoured each booth for all the women's handkerchiefs she could locate, she returned to the register out of breath. If her father had been there, he could have searched the rooms filled with various booths while she continued to cover the front door and register, but he had been gone for well over an hour.

"Is this all you have?" Marian asked.

"They're all the ones I could find." Connie drank from her water bottle.

Ellen counted them out. "These are lovely. Thank you."

Marian pulled two from the pile. "These look too old."

"They're antiques, like we're becoming if you take any longer, Marian." Ellen wore a tight smile.

"Okay. We'll buy all of them."

Connie rang up the sale.

Marian held the package of hankies. "Thanks, Connie. One more thing. Do you know if any of the stores in town carry Erick Sahler prints?"

"Bruder Home does."

"Great. I want to stop by Victorian Charm as well."

As the front door closed behind the women, Connie called her husband's cellphone.

"What's the matter?"

Connie rarely called Jack during the day, so he tended to assume the worst.

"Dad walked out of here this morning, and I haven't seen him since."

"What did you say to him?"

"Why do you always assume it's my fault?"

"Oh, I don't know. Maybe because it usually is."

"I don't have time for the blame game. I want you to find him."

"Did you call his house?"

"Of course. Several times. No answer."

"We have to make him use that cell phone we bought him last Christmas."

"When chicken have teeth."

"Where do you think he went?"

"Well, this might sound crazy, but I think he may be next door."

"So go over and see."

"Not next door to the store. Next door to our house. At Audrey's."

"Why would he be there?"

"I invited her to dinner with Dad at our house before the bathtub races."

"And you told him, and he walked out."

"Exactly."

"So why would he go to her house if he doesn't even want to have dinner with her?"

"How should I know?"

"You're beginning to sound like a screech owl, Connie."

Connie tried to settle herself. "Would you please see if he's at Audrey's?"

"I don't know how to do that without being obvious."

Men, she thought to herself. "I'm really worried about him."

"I think it makes more sense to check his house first. I'll go over there. He's probably taking a nap or something and didn't hear the phone."

"Okay. But if he's not home, call me. I want to know."

Dan stood next to Audrey in her kitchen while she washed two lunch plates and he dried.

"I'm glad you stayed for lunch."

"Me, too."

"We needed to eat something besides peaches and cream pie."

"It's good to be at the age where we can eat dessert first." He opened a cabinet but found glasses in there.

"It's the next one over." She dried her hands. "If I had known, I would have used my better china today, but I haven't finished unpacking everything."

"Is that what's in the boxes in the hall?"

"Yes, along with a few other odds and ends."

"Can I help you unpack?" Dan folded the dish towel over the dish drainer.

"I couldn't ask you to do that."

"You didn't ask. I offered." Dan walked into the hall.

Audrey followed. "But don't you have to get back to the antiques mall?"

"Are you trying to find a nice way to get rid of me?"

"No!" Audrey touched her cheek. "I mean, no, of course not."

"Connie's fine." He scratched his head. "I never imagined I would, but I'm enjoying myself."

Audrey raised her eyebrows. "Good . . . I think."

"That didn't come out right. What I meant was, I'm having a nice time."

"I am as well."

"Which box first?"

"If you're sure, the top one, I guess. Just put it on the kitchen table."

Once the box was settled, and Dan pulled the packing tape off, Audrey lifted out the first dinner plate wrapped in packing paper.

"I guess I should wash these again before I put them away. My mother would have done that."

"Mine, too. And my wife." Dan paused. "Although I'm sure they were clean when you packed them."

Audrey unwrapped the plate.

Without looking at the back of the plate for the pattern name, Dan said, "That's 'Summertime,' introduced by Royal Winton in the thirties. My wife had the entire set."

"I always loved the cheery pink, yellow, and blue flower buds."

"Cheery is exactly right. They were designed to cheer folks up during the Great Depression. Maybe we'd better wash them by hand; they're very delicate."

"Yes. You're right." Audrey filled the sink with soapy water.

Dan unwrapped more china and placed it gently in the sink. "I used to sell whole sets of this stuff, but young people don't seem to want antiques for their wedding china anymore."

"It's a shame. I hope my daughter or one of my granddaughters will take this, but it may end up in your store when I'm gone. However, I do have a grandson who actually loves old things."

Dan rinsed and wiped the first plate dry. "Is he a shipwright?"

"Yes."

"Connie mentioned him. Is he working on the restoration of the *Edna E. Lockwood*?"

"Absolutely. Evan loves old boats and antique furniture, and he might want my china if he ever settles down and gets married."

"It would be nice to give the china to a boy. It always goes to the girls. We only had Connie, so I gave her everything she wanted when my wife passed."

"What was your wife's name?"

"Constance. We always called our daughter Connie, but she's named after her mother."

"Unusual. It's usually the eldest boy who gets his father's name."

"Well, I try not to admit it to Connie, but I was ahead of my time. I always leaned toward liberal ideals and, I guess, feminism. I never saw why women couldn't do what they wanted and have the same privileges as men do."

"Why don't you admit it to your daughter?" Audrey washed another plate.

"I like to get her goat. Keep her on her feet."

"You're an instigator."

Dan grinned. "I suppose I am."

"Tell me about Constance."

"We were high school sweethearts. She had a rough coming up, but she was always positive. Upbeat, you know what I mean?"

Audrey nodded.

"She didn't take any guff off anyone. Smart as a whip. And I loved her cooking, especially her roast pork. And her Thanksgiving chestnut stuffing was amazing." Dan paused. "Tell me about your husband."

"His name was Tom. He was very kind and patient. He was always telling me to simmer down." Audrey laughed.

"How did you meet?"

Audrey continued to wash the unpacked china. "In Korea. He was a helicopter pilot. I was in a MASH unit. Connie told me that you were on the *USS New Jersey* during the Korean War."

"Yes." Dan dried a plate and opened another cabinet. "Are these going in here?"

"Yes. Thank you."

"Hello?" Dan's son-in-law stood awkwardly outside the back door.

Audrey dried her hands and opened the door. "Jack, come on in."

"I rang the bell and knocked out front, but I guess you didn't hear me."

"Connie send you to hunt me down?" Dan asked.

"No," Jack said, but he looked away.

"I'm sorry you had to come around back. My doorbell isn't working, and I guess we were so busy talking, we didn't hear you knock."

"What's wrong with your doorbell?" Dan closed the cabinet door.

"I don't know. It's lost its whatsit, I guess." Audrey turned to Jack. "We just finished lunch, but I can make you a sandwich if you're hungry."

"Dad ate lunch with you?"

"Is there something wrong with that?" Dan snapped.

Jack just put his hands up.

"Audrey, I'll take a look at your doorbell when we're finished getting you unpacked."

"Thank you, Dan."

"Well, I'll just be on my way." Jack lumbered toward the back door.

"Did you want something, Jack?" Audrey asked.

"Um." Jack looked at his father-in-law and then back at the new neighbor. "Yes. Would you two prefer grilled salmon or steaks before the bathtub races?"

"Salmon, please. What can I bring? I make a pretty mean peaches and cream pie." Audrey winked at Dan.

He turned to his son-in-law. "I'd like a steak, Jack. If you don't mind."

"Fine. I'll make sure we have plenty of both. Thank you for offering to make a pie. Connie will appreciate that." Jack opened the back door. "Do you want a ride back into town, Dad?"

"No. I'm going to finish helping Audrey."

"Okay." Jack whistled a tune as he walked out to his car.

"I wouldn't have believed it if I hadn't seen it with my own two eyes." Jack leaned against the register counter at the antiques mall.

"Dad was actually helping Audrey unpack?" Connie couldn't contain her enthusiasm.

"They had eaten lunch together, and he was offering to fix her doorbell." Jack laughed.

"This is amazingly wonderful. Even though Dad would deny it, he's been terribly lonely. They have so much in common."

"They seemed to be getting along famously. Oh, Audrey is bringing dessert to our house next week."

"I can assume Dad will be there, too?"

"I would say so. Hey, how about if I help you close up here

and the two of us go to Blacksmith for a bite to eat?"

Connie hugged her husband. "That would be very romantic. It's time we concentrated on the two of us."

"You'd be proud of how I marched right in there to find out what was going on."

"I am proud. Thanks for finding Dad. It ended up much better than I imagined."

Connie's cell phone pinged.

"You've got a text." Jack handed her the phone from the counter.

"It's from Dad!"

"He doesn't know how to text. I didn't even think he carried that cell."

Connie read the text out loud. "Audrey is teaching me how to text. I'm sorry I walked out on you. Were you very busy?"

Connie texted back, "I am sorry I pushed you so much. I didn't mean to upset you."

A moment later, she saw another text. "That's OK. I like Audrey. She makes a mean peaches and cream pie ☺."

Drama Queen

PHILLIP

I'VE ALWAYS LIKED WOMEN, but not for the usual reasons men like them. The girls didn't want to beat me up when I was a kid; they wanted to dress me up in their clothes and put lipstick on me. The boys, however, did want to beat me up and did so every chance they could. Perhaps it's no surprise, then, that my best friend is a woman.

When I should have gotten off the Eastern Shore for college, I instead went to Washington College here in Chestertown, where again, I pretty much stood out as weird. Although I was able to stand up for myself by then, it was comforting when Kate accepted me. We became best friends the first week of freshman year and remained so all through college and into adulthood. It's hard to believe we graduated nearly forty years ago; I haven't aged at all. I can't wait for that reunion. It will take a dancing bear carrying a blow torch to get Kate off her couch to go to the reunion with me, but first things first.

Kate's been hibernating ever since Brad the Bastard left her for a younger woman a few months ago. Talk about stereotypes. Anyway, I've gotten Kate to agree to meet me for lunch today at The Kitchen at the Imperial Hotel. I'll ply her with expensive wine before springing my plan for her relaunching. She's going to fight me. I'd be worried if she didn't. Her resistance will prove to me that she really hasn't given up. I'm ready. I've moved mountains before with her; I can do it again.

When Kate arrives, I ask the hostess to seat us someplace quiet and private. She leads us down the hall, past the crowded dining rooms and out to the garden seating.

"It's too hot out here," Kate complains.

That's just the point. It won't get crowded. But I say, "You need some sun. You're too pale from hiding inside your house."

"I haven't been hiding. I've gone to work every day."

"Inside. You need some air. Get some color back into those lifeless cheeks." I pinch her face.

"Okay." She slaps my hands away and takes a seat. "I didn't come here to argue."

The hostess leaves us with menus. I think she's glad to get away.

"Don't let me order dessert." Kate pats her tummy.

"Get whatever you want."

"No, I've been eating too much. I need to cut back."

"I hope you'll drink some wine."

"Are you kidding? Wine doesn't count; everyone knows that."

"Good." I pick up the wine list to make a selection. Something dry and refreshing.

Kate shuts her menu. "I'm going to order a salad so I can have dessert."

I look over the menu. "I'm going to order an oyster po' boy so I can have potato salad."

Kate looks me over. "You never gain weight."

"High metabolism, I guess."

"I hate you." She smirks and reopens her menu. "But yum, that does sound good."

I keep my mouth shut. Kate always looks lovely. Brad the Bastard is an idiot.

She snaps the menu shut. "Nope. I'm sticking with a salad

because the chocolate bread pudding is calling my name."

"Whatever makes you happy."

The waitress arrives, takes our orders, and returns with the wine. Once Kate has a few sips, she begins to relax.

"Thanks for getting me out of the house, Phillip. I feel better."

"I'm glad."

"Tell me how plans are coming for your niece's wedding."

"Chelsea has approved my design and the fabric for her bridal gown. My sister and her pushy friend, who is also the mother of the groom, tried to influence Chelsea's decisions, but I kept her on the right track. It's going to be stunning."

"How exciting for her to have an uncle who is an award-winning Broadway costume designer. I hope she realizes how lucky she is that you're doing her gown."

"I love all my nieces to pieces, and my retirement from full-time work in New York has given me the time to make Chelsea's wedding gown. I'm delighted." This is the perfect segue into my plan of action for Kate. "I plan to keep busy. I'll be designing the costumes for *Sweeney Todd* at the Garfield Center. They're holding auditions soon."

"I love Stephen Sondheim musicals."

Our food arrives, and I pause from my strategy to try my oyster sandwich. "Oh my God, you have to have a bite of this."

"No, thanks." Kate stabs at her salad. "Brad and I saw the production of an Edward Albee play that the Garfield did a couple of years ago. It was depressing but well done."

"Albee plays are always depressing. They ought to put a suicide hotline number in the program."

"What was the name of that play? Not *Who's Afraid of Virginia Woolf.* Talk about torture. People yelling at each other for over two hours. If I wanted that, I could have just stayed home with Brad for the evening." She takes a swallow of wine. "But I like most of Albee's other plays."

"I hate to admit it, but I do, too. It must say something about our need for psychological torment."

"Probably." Kate smiles. "*Seascape* is one of my favorites."

"I'd die to design the lizard costumes for it, but no one's going to do an absurdist play on the Eastern Shore, not even here in Chestertown. Two lizards talking to humans on a beach? Please." I sigh. "Sometimes I miss New York."

"*A Delicate Balance.* That's the one we saw."

"More wine?" I ask.

"No, I'd better stop." She drinks some of her ice water.

Kate and I had done a few shows together in college, so while she is enjoying her salad, I decide to bring them up first. "You were so good in the plays back in college."

After finishing a bite of lettuce, Kate says, "That was a long time ago. The most fun was when you and I were in Moliere's *The Imaginary Invalid.*"

"Your Toinette was brilliantly funny."

She dismisses me with a wave of her hand. "Only because I was playing opposite you as Argon. Your curtain call started a standing ovation every night. People were practically peeing themselves from laughing at your imaginary ailments. But Lord, those rhyming couplets. I thought I'd go mad."

"You had such a nice singing voice, too."

Kate eyes me, and I realize she's catching on.

"Why are you bringing this up?"

"No reason. It's just nice to reminisce."

Kate sighs. "I wish I knew then what I know now."

It seems I must circle around a bit. "What would you do differently?"

"Not marry Brad."

"It was good for a while."

"Well, I don't really mean that. He gave me four wonderful children, who are all launched and successful. Hopefully, someday I'll be a grandmother. Still, his leaving makes me feel nothing like my adorable, petite, energetic Toinette. Now I'm more like a frump. A failure. A frumpy failure."

"Stop putting yourself down. You're still beautiful."

"Thank you." She finishes her salad and drinks more water.

"When we were kids, you were the only woman I would have jumped the fence for."

Kate snorts. "I'm not complimented. You slept with anyone or anything that was willing."

"Well, you should be complimented. Besides, I was only screwing around with anyone and everyone back then because I was trying to figure out who I was."

"Thank God we never had sex. I don't know if we would have been able to remain friends."

"Of course we would. We're bosom buddies." I start to sing "We'll Always Be Bosom Buddies" from *Mame*, but I don't get very far.

"You don't have a bosom."

"That depends on what I'm wearing." I wave my napkin dramatically.

She laughs.

I get serious. "Kate, don't you think it's time you start rebuilding your life?"

"I don't feel like it." She shifts in her chair. "All the men you've been through, and you never found Mr. Right. And look at my older sister, Trudy. She never found Mr. Right, and she's more beautiful than I am."

"I'm not talking about you dating. Not yet anyway." I decide it's time to play hardball. "You're such a drama queen, acting like you're the first woman to lose a husband to a younger woman."

"The bimbo is only five years younger than I am."

"Not exactly a spring chicken." I pour myself more wine.

"But she's got something I don't."

"Yes, an ass for a new partner. Your loss is her loss. No one gains here."

"Except Brad. He gets to start all over with a new, younger model."

"You just said she wasn't that much younger. Anyway, you get to start over, too—if you ever give yourself the chance. I think auditioning for *Sweeney Todd* is the perfect way to do that."

"I knew you weren't bringing up my distant, short-lived jaunt on stage for no reason. Well, I'm not doing it."

"Yes, you are." I refill Kate's wine glass. "I already signed you up."

"How dare you!"

"There's the drama queen again. Did you even consider that's the reason Brad the Bastard moved on?"

"Oh, please." Kate takes a long sip of wine.

"Auditions are a few weeks away. We need to find a monologue and sixteen bars of a song for you to do."

"I haven't sung in a million years."

"That's okay. Mrs. Lovett isn't that big of a singing role. Angela Lansbury talked her way through half the songs and won another Tony."

"They aren't going to give a lead to someone who's never worked with them. They have a dozen regulars going for that role."

"How do you know that?"

"I ought to just audition for the chorus."

"So you're going to do it?"

"If I do, it's only to shut you up. Once you get an idea in your head, there's no living with you until you get your way."

I have her right where I want her. "You're right. Maybe you should just audition for the chorus."

"Are you saying I'm only good enough to be in the chorus?"

"Don't put words in my mouth." The waitress returns to take our plates and offer us dessert.

"No, thanks," Kate says.

I turn to her in surprise. "I thought you wanted the chocolate bread pudding."

"That was before I was considering going back on stage."

"That's my girl. We'll start rehearsing for your audition next week."

"I said 'considering.'" Kate folds her napkin and places it on the table. "And what do you mean 'we'?"

"You don't think you're going to do this on your own, do you?"

"Apparently not."

"I'm going to coach you."

"Phillip, I know you mean well, but I'm not sure about this." Kate gets up from the table and kisses my cheek. "I have to give this some serious thought."

"Text me."

She walks away, but I know she'll come around. My plan is working, and I might as well begin celebrating now. I pour another glass of wine and order the chocolate bread pudding.

KATE

On my way to the Garfield Center for the Arts, my palms begin to sweat. The theatre is next door to the restaurant where Phillip first told me about his harebrained idea to have me audition. As usual in our friendship, I caved to his persistence, and now I really have to do it. I think about going home, but I know Phillip will kill me. He spent so much time helping me prepare. I owe it to him to at least audition, even if I make a fool of myself.

Inside the lobby, I am handed an audition form to fill out. Phillip advised me to check off both "Mrs. Lovett" and "I'll accept any role." My hand shakes as I complete the form. People are quietly milling around, but a soprano is vocalizing in the ladies room. I think you can hear her clear down to the Chester River.

A man bounds through the theatre doors and into the lobby. "Would someone tell that woman to shut up? We can't hear the auditions on stage." He quickly disappears back into the theatre.

The woman collecting completed audition forms rushes into the ladies room. I wouldn't want to be whoever is in there warming up.

I can't sit still, so I keep pacing and take some deep breaths. I run through my monologue again. I hum to keep my voice warmed up because I'm less confident about my singing.

After the soprano blows out the theatre walls during her audition, the man comes out again. "Kate Nicoli."

My heart leaps into my throat, and I'm not sure I can breathe, let alone speak and sing.

I silently follow him into the house. The director and other production members are sitting in the back where I have to walk past them.

"Please give your music to the accompanist." The man points to the woman sitting at the piano near the stage.

I walk down and hand her my music, which is in a plastic sleeve, making it easier to turn. "Hi. I'm doing these sixteen bars." I point to the pickup spot on the music. "The sixteen bars end here."

"It's nearly the end of the song. I'll play out so you have a big finish." She smiles.

"Thank you."

"Are you doing the song or monologue first?" she asks.

"Monologue."

"Good luck."

As I go up on stage, I smile and stand up straight. Phillip had said, "It's important to be friendly and confident. They want to cast someone reliable and easy to work with. No drama queens."

I look at the production team. "Hello, my name is Kate Nicoli. My monologue is from *Noises Off*, and my song is "So Long, Dearie" from *Hello, Dolly.*"

I slouch and adjust my voice to be more nasal. During the monologue, I hear them laughing, and I feel adrenalin coursing through me.

That was the easy part. Now I have to sing. I close my eyes briefly and take a full breath. *Treat it like a monologue*, I hear Phillip say in my head. I open my eyes and nod to the woman at the piano. She plays a brief introduction leading into the section I chose to sing. Just as Phillip coached me to do, I picture my ex in the back row of the theatre and I sing to him/Horace about how much he'll regret leaving/not marrying me. They laugh again when I sing that he can snuggle up to his cash register. It feels good to be in control of my audition. I'm genuinely having fun.

"Could you sing something with a cockney accent?"

Damn. That Phillip is always right. He'd made me learn "Just You Wait" from *My Fair Lady* because, although Eliza Doolittle isn't the right age for me to play, she has a strong cockney accent.

"Yes." I walk to the foot of the stage and speak to the accompanist. "In the other sleeve I left next to you is "Just You Wait.""

"Great choice," she says.

Again I picture Brad, and I feel a great deal of frustration and indignation as I tell him how when he's sick, I won't take care of him. Hell, I had no idea how convenient my ex-husband could become.

When I finish singing, the director asks, "Can you stay for callbacks for Mrs. Lovett later this evening?"

"Absolutely." I smile. "Thank you."

My mouth is completely dry by the time I reach the water fountain in the lobby. I know that Phillip is waiting on pins and needles, so I text him that I made callbacks. He texts back that he isn't surprised and that I must come over afterwards.

Phillip taught me all of Mrs. Lovett's songs, but I don't have anything memorized. He told me it wasn't necessary because if I make it to callbacks, they expect me to hold the music. Still, I don't feel as prepared. I try not to drive myself around the bend worrying while I wait nearly two hours before callbacks begin.

Everyone being considered for principal roles is in the theatre gathered around the piano. I am one of three women they are considering for Mrs. Lovett. I sing part of "By the Sea," and then each of them sings the same section. After we sing, they have two gentlemen sing for Sweeney, and three young women sing for Joanna. The loud soprano is one of them, and she is less nervous and more in control of her voice. They work through all the lead roles, and finally each of the Mrs. Lovetts sings part of the duet with the two Sweeney Todds.

When we are done, the production team speaks in hushed tones in the back of the house. Then we are thanked and told they'll be calling people later tonight, so make sure to have our cell phone numbers on the forms we completed.

One of the possible Mrs. Lovetts approaches me. "I think you've got the role. You were wonderful."

I give her a hug. "So were you. Time will tell."

I head out into the warm night air and drive directly to Phillip's. Being cast or not, I feel like I've accomplished something very important. Even if my ex-husband fueled part of my audition, I have begun a life without Brad.

"Darling!" Phillip greets me with a hug and a glass of wine.

"Tell me everything."

We sit in his garden room where a rather lazy ceiling fan just makes it comfortable.

"I couldn't have done this without your coaching, Phillip. I did everything you said to do. When they began laughing during my monologue, it gave me a huge surge of confidence."

He smiles knowingly. "I think you're going to get Lovett."

"Don't say that. You'll jinx it."

"Are you hungry?"

"Starving, but I have to lose some weight if I'm going back on stage."

Phillip waves his hand and disappears into the house. When he returns, he's carrying a plate of sliced fresh vegetables.

"You're an angel." I start munching.

"Was it cut-throat?" He sips his wine.

"Not at all. Everyone was very supportive of one another. I honestly want to work with this cast even if I'm on the prop crew."

My cell rings. I look at Phillip. "Answer it for me."

"I will not." He waits, but I'm frozen with fear. "For God's sake!" Phillip grabs my phone. "Hello?" He listens. "It's Phillip, but Kate's right here."

I feel about to cry.

"Okay." Phillip whispers to me, "It's the director. She wants to know if you'd like to do Mrs. Lovett."

I scream, "Give me that." I grab the phone. "Yes! I'd love to take the role of Mrs. Lovett."

The director laughs. "That's wonderful. I'm so glad to have you on board. So how long have you known Phillip?"

"Since college."

"We're lucky to have someone of his caliber designing the costumes."

I can't catch my breath and think I may be about to have a heart attack.

"Kate? Are you still there?" she asks.

"Yes, I am."

"You'll get an email tomorrow with the rehearsal schedule and answers to a lot of your questions."

"Thank you so much!"

"Thank you for taking the role." She ends the call.

I look at Phillip with tears pooling in my eyes.

He kisses my hand. "I'd say that champagne is in order!"

CRAB CAKE TANGO

THINKING ABOUT CRAB CAKES for dinner was nothing new for me. Eastern Shore natives set their clocks according to when crabs are running, but I had had crab cakes on my mind all day. Folks around here can argue for days about which local chef did up the best crab cakes, so I made it my business to sample every crab cake within twenty miles of Cambridge, and then some. At three o'clock, I'd phoned in my six o'clock pickup order for some big boys with coleslaw and pickled beets. Soon I'd be initiating my Friday night with crab cakes and a glass of wine, followed by a good book. Heaven.

With the weekend soon to commence, there had been no lull in the line of customers waiting to have their hair cut at the Cambridge Creek Barbershop. I didn't take appointments. Gentlemen just popped in whenever it was convenient, and today seemed to have been convenient for nearly everyone in town. I finished Rick Happerman's haircut and prepared him for a shave.

"I don't know about trusting a woman with a straight-edge razor on my throat," Rick teased, as he often did.

"Rick, in all these years, have I ever cut you?"

"No, but there's a first time for everything, Trudy."

"Hush up, or I might just do it today." I had to pause while he chuckled.

Angie Dodge sat waiting with her dad. His mind was slipping away from dementia, but he still knew who I was. "Prettiest barber I've ever seen," he always said.

"That's not saying much, Clive, since I'm the only lady barber you've ever seen," I always replied, and he'd laugh and pat my hand. My favorite part came next: "You're beautiful, Trudy."

I was finishing Rick when the bell rang on my shop door. In strolled Hugh Jackman. Not *the* Hugh Jackman, but *our* Hugh Jackman. I glanced at the clock—5:05. This would make getting to my six o'clock pick-up awfully tight. I'd sacrifice crab cakes if *the* Hugh Jackman came sauntering in for a haircut, but for *our* Hugh Jackman? Who am I kidding? I've never disappointed a customer.

"Hey, Trudy," Hugh greeted me before saying hello to Angie and her dad.

"How much do you need, Hugh?" I turned Rick loose.

"Just a trim." Hugh shook hands with Rick. "My wife decided to have her parents over for dinner at the last minute. I don't want to listen to my mother-in-law complain about my hair hittin' my shirt collar."

"Okay. I can manage that if you can wait a few minutes." I took Clive by the hand and led him over to the chair. "Let's take care of you next, okay?"

The fragile gentleman looked a little unsure.

"Trudy is going to give you a haircut, Dad," Angie patiently reassured her father, as she probably did about a million times a day.

"That would be nice." When I turned his chair to face the mirror, his eyes caught mine. "You're the prettiest barber I've ever seen."

I ran a comb through his hair. "That's not saying much, Clive, since I'm the only lady barber you've ever seen."

He patted my hand. "You're beautiful, Trisha."

Angie and I glanced at one another.. She had stopped correcting him a while back. It only confused him more. I didn't care what name he called me as long as he said I was beautiful.

As Hugh and Angie chatted, I gave Clive his usual cut. Angie had warned me a long time ago not to try to change anything. Consistency helped keep her dad calm. Despite my no-appointments policy, I knew to expect Angie and Clive on the second Friday afternoon of every month. During the last few years, if their date hit a holiday, I still came in just for Clive.

Angie and I weren't close, but we had graduated high school together in 1973. She was a local like me. Her father had been a waterman. When Clive first began to get confused, the family worried that he'd get lost out on the bay he once knew like the back of his hand. Angie's brother switched to night shift at the hospital so he could go out with his dad in the morning. But when Clive really began to decline, he had to be grounded. I admired how patient Angie was with her father. I know I'd rather have any other disease. To be robbed of one's mind must be pure hell.

By the time I wrapped up with Hugh, I only had five minutes to drive over to pick up my dinner. My mouth was watering when I parked on Trenton Street and dashed into the restaurant.

"Table for one?" The young hostess smiled in a genuine manner.

"Are you new here?" I asked.

"Yes, just started."

"Good luck. It's a great place."

"I like it so far. Do you want to sit inside or out?"

"Oh, I'm here to pick up a take-out order for Trudy. That's me."

The girl looked confused. I figured she hadn't been on the job long enough to know what to do for a pick-up. I waited.

"Um. Just a minute." She walked back toward the kitchen.

Two couples arrived, and since there was no one to seat them, I said, "She'll be right back."

"No problem. We're in no hurry," one of the men said.

A few minutes later, a family of five came through the door.

"I can't imagine what's keeping her." I began tapping my foot and then forced myself to stop.

Ken, the manager, arrived, trailing after the young hostess. She took the two couples toward the tables on the deck.

"Hi, Trudy."

I shook Ken's hand. "How are you doing?" He'd just been in for a haircut last week.

"Fine."

"I forgot to ask about your children when you were in."

"Everyone is good. The oldest is going into high school this fall."

"How is that possible?"

The father of the family of five cleared his throat. Obviously a tourist. When people on the shore talked to one another, everything else just ground to a halt. We were all used to it and wouldn't want it any other way.

"The hostess will seat you in just a moment." Ken pulled me aside. "Trudy, we don't have a take-out order for you. We haven't gotten any calls for takeout tonight."

"But I called around three this afternoon."

"Do you know who you talked to?" Ken was trying to help, but I began to feel anxious.

"I don't know. One of the kids."

"Male or female?"

"Male."

"None of the guys were in that early. Melissa has been on shift since two, but she's only gotten calls for reservations."

"And we have one." The mother stepped forward. "It was for six o'clock."

Just then, Melissa returned. "Can I help you?"

"Roberts. Reservation for five."

"Right this way."

After they trooped off, I looked at Ken. "My God, what is it like when you're really jammed up?"

"Some people are always in a rush. Now, back to your takeout. What did you order?"

"Jumbo crab cakes with coleslaw and pickled beets."

"And you're sure you called here?"

"Of course." I was beginning to lose my patience as a party of four thirty-somethings arrived.

"Maybe you called someplace else and thought you called here."

I whispered in hopes that the customers behind me wouldn't hear me. "That's ridiculous. Why would I do that? I know I called River View."

"You're at Portside."

"Well, of course I am."

"But you said that you called River View."

"Oh, my God." I could feel my face begin to heat up. "Ken, I'm so sorry."

"Not to worry, Trudy. Portside. River View. They're very similar."

He was trying to make me feel better, but I only felt worse. I'd lived here my entire life. I knew perfectly well where every restaurant, store, and business was located. I'm an active member of the Chamber of Commerce, for God's sake.

"Would you like me to put the order in for you now? You can wait in the bar. I'll buy you a drink."

"No, Ken. Thank you for the offer. I can't leave River View with an entire meal waiting to be picked up. I'll just drive on over there now." I looked at my watch. "Half an hour late."

"Okay, Trudy. We'll see you next time."

"Thanks, Ken." I rushed past the young people waiting to be

seated, feeling their eyes on me. *You just wait another thirty years*, I thought to myself. *You won't think it's so funny then.*

When I had to think about where I parked my car and where my keys were, my head began to pound. I turned on my car engine and put the air conditioning on full blast. How could I have called River View, which is way out on the highway, driven to Portside, which is in town, and expected them to have my damn crab cakes? I really just wanted to go home and curl up in my bed, but later I'd hear about how I never picked up my order. Cambridge was bigger than other Eastern Shore towns, but everyone still knew everything about everybody. I gripped the steering wheel. "I hope I can find the way," I muttered to myself.

When I arrived at River View at the Point, the parking lot was jammed. I circled around and scored an open spot next to a blue Jeep Renegade. I grabbed my purse, stepped out of my Honda, rounded the corner of the Jeep, and nearly ran into a man carrying a take-out bag. About my age, he had long, salt-and-pepper hair pulled back in a ponytail. He smiled at me with straight, white teeth, but what hit me was how his weathered skin wrinkled around his gray eyes. This guy was way too appealing for my own good. I nodded and skirted past him up to the restaurant.

At the entry to the restaurant, a man was negotiating an older woman's wheelchair through the entrance while an elderly gentleman held the door open. I guessed it was an adult son and his parents. The father said, "Sorry to hold you up."

"It's no problem." I was so late now, what could it matter.

They were just moving out of my way when I saw the Jeep drive by with the take-out bag perched on the roof.

"You forgot your food," I yelled, waving to the driver and pointing to the bag on the roof.

The door to the restaurant swung closed as I watched the man stop, hop out, glance at the bag, and then turn. He walked toward me. "Aren't you Trudy Benson? I'm Sam Woodrich. We went to high school together."

"Sam?" I could see it now. He had been cute in school, but time had been good to him. I hate men. They always age better than women, at least this woman.

"Trudy, you look wonderful." He gave me a quick hug.

Well, maybe I hadn't completely fallen apart. That, or he needed glasses.

"Thanks, Sam. You've held up well, too."

That smile again with the adorable crow's-feet.

"It's been a long time."

"Didn't you move to California?" I asked.

"I did. Spent my career out there working for various vineyards."

"What are you doing here in Cambridge?" I must have sounded positively giddy to see him. What the hell?

"I retired, but I'm consulting now. Start-up vineyards hire me to train their staffs and teach them what equipment to purchase."

"Heaven knows they're booming around here."

"Exactly. Maryland vineyards are beginning to be recognized."

"So you're here on a consulting job?"

"I've moved back. I just bought a place."

"Really!" I wasn't sure why I felt so happy about that. After a near-miss in my twenties, I have lived the single life. I always kept my relationships casual. Men were great up to a point. Put too much faith in them, and your heart gets broken. My sister is the perfect example. Her husband recently left her after thirty-six years of marriage and raising four children. No, I don't need it. It would be best if Sam went on his way. "Your food is getting cold."

He actually blushed. "I was so distracted by you that I forgot to put it in the car after fishing around in my pockets for my keys."

"Join the club."

"What did you forget?"

"Nothing. I'll tell you later." Why did I just say that?

"Do you have someone waiting for you inside?"

I thought about saying yes, but there was something happening here that I couldn't put my finger on.

"Ms. Benson?" a youthful male voice called from the restaurant entrance.

I turned around. "Yes?" I couldn't grasp why anyone would be calling my name.

A tall, young man walked over to us. "I'm Chris Jackman. My dad is Hugh."

I finally recognized him. "Yes. Of course. How are you?"

"I'm fine, ma'am. I took your order for the jumbo crab cakes this afternoon. I just noticed you out here and wondered if you wanted me to have them heated up again."

"I apologize for being so late."

"Cold crab cakes don't sound very appealing. Why don't we go inside for dinner and catch up?" Sam suggested. "Mine are probably cold, too." He gestured over his shoulder with his thumb.

"That would be such a waste." Now I sounded like some old biddy who counted her pennies.

"Ms. Benson, I apologize, but I have to get back inside to work."

Eating dinner with Sam would feel too much like a date. He was likely married. I glanced down to make sure but saw no ring.

Sam must have sensed my hesitation. "Or we could have our dinners reheated and have a picnic down on the waterfront."

"Okay," I heard myself say. Two old high school friends catching up in the park seemed innocent enough.

"Great. I'll meet you at Sailwinds Park. I'll pick up something for us to drink." Sam turned to the young man. "Chris, would you please reheat our food and give Ms. Benson extra plastic forks and napkins?"

"Yes, sir."

"I'll see you shortly." Sam dashed to his Jeep, nearly forgetting his dinner again, laughed, and grabbed it off the roof to give to Chris.

I followed Chris inside to pay for my takeout.

When I reached Sailwinds Park, I parked next to Sam's Jeep. I scanned the park and saw him waving from a picnic table where he had opened a bottle of white wine and set out two plastic wine glasses. As I carried our dinners over, I wondered why I had agreed to this.

Closer to the water, a breeze off the Choptank River caught the loose ends of my hair. I had just brushed it at a red light, but it was a relief to be cooled off.

Sam stood. "I hope you like this French pinot blanc. It has a light touch of almond, apple, and spice that should go well with our crab cakes."

"You got them, too?"

He grinned. "I went overboard with French fries. I picked up some bottled water, if you don't care for wine."

"Thank you, I'd love some wine." I tried to gracefully lift one leg over the affixed bench and then the other. It was always an accomplishment to get into one of these picnic tables.

For several moments, we organized our dinners, ate a little, and sipped some wine. We watched the various workboats and pleasure crafts out on the river.

"Didn't you marry Larry Powers?" Sam asked between bites of his crab cakes. "You were together through most of high school."

I swallowed some coleslaw. "I nearly did. Managed to dodge that bullet at the last minute."

"What happened?"

"Larry was an ass."

Sam laughed. "I could have told you that."

"Why didn't you?"

"You wouldn't have listened to me." Sam gobbled up a French fry.

"Not in high school, no. I thought I was in love." I rolled my eyes to accentuate my point.

"I wanted to ask you to prom, but you were going steady with Larry."

"I wish you had. Maybe I would have realized sooner that I was wasting my time." I waved a fly away from my second crab cake. "After we graduated, I grew up, but Larry didn't. I wanted to travel, and I became politically aware. I enjoyed reading and art. Larry didn't care about anything that would be considered self-improvement. He thought he was perfect."

Sam laughed again. I loved how his smile traveled all the way up to his eyes. He had no right to be this adorable.

"Did you ever marry?" he asked.

"No. I began to like my independence. How about you?"

"Yes. Divorced."

"Sorry. Any kids?" I took another bite of my crab cake.

"No. That became the issue. I wanted a family, but she was satisfied with her career. We parted amicably."

I shook my head. "And you never married again?"

"No. I ended up traveling a lot for my work." He took a sip of wine. "I felt too hurt to trust anyone again, and by the time I got over it, other things were taking priority."

His vulnerability touched me. He had always been genuine. I was glad that hadn't changed. "I'm sorry that you never got to have children. I think you would have been a good parent."

"Thanks. I'm at peace with it. Besides, I've been a very involved uncle and a godfather to three kids. Now those youngsters are getting married and having babies. It's worked out."

"I love being an aunt. My sister, Kate, had four children, and I hope for grandnieces or grandnephews eventually."

"I remember Kate. She was a couple of years behind us, right?"

"Yes."

"How is she?"

I took a moment to wipe my hands on one of the napkins. "Not so great, recently. Her husband ended the marriage."

"How sad."

"It's pretty ugly. I really feel for her."

"I'm sorry." I could see real empathy in Sam's expression.

"But Kate will land on her feet. She always does." This was getting depressing, so I shifted the topic. "You said you traveled with your work."

Sam finished his last fry. "Yes. I spent most of my time in France, Spain, and Italy."

"I love Paris. It's truly a beautiful city."

"Have you been to Barcelona?" he asked.

"No. It's on the bucket list."

"Good. You don't want to miss that. Where else have you been?"

"Do you mind if we stretch our legs?" I stood up and began the procedure of untangling myself from the picnic table. "I'm getting stiff."

"Me, too." Sam stood and stretched his arms. I wondered what it might be like to be in those arms.

We deposited our trash in a nearby receptacle. Sam poured more wine in our glasses and we carried them out along the dock, which gave us a lovely view of the Choptank River Lighthouse.

"Let's see. I've been to England, France, Scotland, and Italy. I've also visited forty of the fifty states. Oh, and I went to Iceland to see the Northern Lights."

"Now that's on *my* bucket list." Sam held his half-full, plastic wine glass. "Let's toast to more world travels."

I gently touched my glass to his. I'd traveled alone or with girlfriends and gone on a few Rick Steves' Tours. My imagination was working on overload, picturing what it would be like to travel with Sam instead. These thoughts were unnerving me.

"Listen, I'd better get going." I had no excuse, so I left it at that.

He didn't argue or ask any questions. "Let's start back to our cars, and on the way, you can tell me what you forgot."

"Oh."

"You promised. It can't be more embarrassing than driving away with a dinner on the roof of your car."

I finished my wine. "It's too mortifying to tell you."

"Oh, come on." He smiled again, which turned me into a puddle.

"All right. But this stays between us."

"Scout's honor."

"Okay. Here goes. I ordered my dinner at the wrong place. I called River View when I meant to call Portside."

Sam chuckled. "That's not so bad."

"It gets worse." We arrived back at the picnic table. "I went to Portside and insisted that they had a take-out dinner for me. When the manager and I figured out what I had done, I wanted to cry. I have a client with dementia. It scares the crap out of me."

"I believe that if you just can't find your keys, you're okay. It's when you forget what the keys are for that you have to worry."

"It's been quite a night." I took a swig of water from the bottle I had opened before.

"It sure has been for me. I'm glad you went to the wrong place first for your crab cakes, Trudy."

"Why?"

"Because it meant you'd be at the right restaurant when I came out so we could run into each other."

"That's true." I wanted to add that I was glad it had happened, but something kept me from revealing too much.

We tossed our plastic wine glasses in a nearby bin and walked to our cars.

"What kind of a client is this gentleman with the dementia?" Sam asked.

"I'm a barber."

"How cool is that. A lady barber."

"I'm the only one around. It's kind of fun being a novelty. My shop is right in town. The Cambridge Creek Barbershop." I unlocked my car, and Sam opened my door. He smelled like citrus and bay air. "Why did you move back here?"

"It was time to come home. I hadn't planned to stay on the West Coast all those years. Something was always pulling me back here."

I looked out at the river. "I love to travel and visit other places, but I couldn't leave."

"I'm here to stay."

I got into my car. "Thanks, Sam. This was fun."

"Trudy, I'd like to see you again."

"Tomorrow is Second Saturday. The shop will be open after hours. We'll have wine and cheese. Kate is coming down. Stop by if you're around."

"That would be a great way to start." He shut my door.

As I pulled away, I thought, *Start what?* I found myself humming the entire drive home.

LEAPS OF FAITH

S I DRIVE SOUTH on Route 50, I feel annoying butterflies in the pit of my stomach. My sister, Trudy, doesn't need any help setting up for Second Saturday at her Cambridge barbershop. She's begged me to come down from Chestertown and to stay overnight because she thinks I'm still having trouble coming to terms with Brad ending our marriage, and to some extent, she's right. Being cast in *Sweeney Todd* has given me quite a lift, but now I'm plagued with misgivings. What was I thinking when I accepted the role of Mrs. Lovett? I wasn't thinking. I must have been temporarily insane to consider going back on stage.

When I drive over Cambridge Creek on the Market Street Bridge, I decide to start looking for a parking spot up on High Street. Already the sidewalks are beginning to fill with folks out for Second Saturday when the shops and galleries stay open late and offer complimentary wine and appetizers. There's no parking anywhere near the Dorchester Center for the Arts, which is lit up like a Christmas tree. I turn onto Race Street, and miraculously, someone is vacating a spot in front of Craig's Drug Store, across and up the street from the Cambridge Creek Barbershop. I gather up two bags full of wine and cheeses and hurry along to my sister's establishment.

I pause for a moment outside and watch Trudy through one of the two large storefront windows she's filled with charming antiques and decorative lights. It's one thing to know how to cut hair. It's another to be able to build a successful business as a female barber. I can't help but smile in admiration. My sister is sweeping the floor around her barber chair when I barrel in the door carrying her Second Saturday goodies.

"You look great, Kate." She washes her hands in the sink. "Your hair is shorter."

"You like it?" Although she cuts men's hair, she did my hair once, right after completing her training. We argued so much during the process that I never asked again. Still, I care about her professional opinion.

She orders me to spin around with the flick of her finger. I put the bags down and turn.

"I do. It's sassy." She pulls her shoulder-length hair out of a hair band. It's a lovely mix of blonde and silver, so she doesn't color it. "I haven't seen that outfit, have I?"

"It's new. I found it at Twigs and Teacups in C-Town."

"Your energy is different." We begin setting up a table where we'll put the refreshments. "What's happened?" Trudy asks.

I giggle while arranging cheeses on the platter Trudy brought from home. "I auditioned for Mrs. Lovett in *Sweeney Todd* at the Garfield Center."

She stops working. "Get out. That's wonderful."

"Phillip suggested it and helped me prepare my monologue and song."

"It's a shame you're not a gay man or that Phillip doesn't prefer women. Either way, he'd be a great match for you. I always liked him better than your soon-to-be ex-husband."

"He's a lot more fun, that's for sure." I arrange small plastic glasses on the table.

"You were good on stage in college. I always wondered why you didn't continue with it."

"Marriage, kids, you know. Brad was never too crazy about me running off to rehearsals." A thought strikes me. "I'm beginning to think he did me a favor by leaving. It's like the entire world has opened up."

Trudy sets out festive napkins. "I'm glad to hear you talking this way. I was a little worried there."

"Me, too. I'm feeling much better now."

My sister nibbles on a slice of cheese. "This is delicious. Try some."

"No cheese for me tonight. I'm trying to lose a few pounds in case I decide to do the role."

Trudy freezes. "Wait. They've already offered you the part?"

"Yes."

"Why the hell didn't you lead with that?" Trudy hugs me. "Congratulations!"

"Thank you, but—"

"Don't tell me you're getting cold feet?" Trudy shakes her finger at me like she did when we were kids.

I feel a lump in my throat. "I was thrilled at first, but I'm beginning to panic now that we're getting close to the first rehearsal."

"Which is when?" Her voice is stern.

"Next week," I squeak.

"Kate!"

"But what if I bomb? What if I forget my lines? What if I can't sing the songs well enough?"

"What if you're brilliant? What if you kick ass as Mrs. Lovett? Did you even consider those 'What ifs'?"

"Hey, enough about me; what's new with you?"

"You've accepted the part. They are counting on you, so you should follow through." She disappears into the back room.

In a desperate attempt to stop talking about my possible public humiliation, I say, "I think you're avoiding my question. What's happening with you?"

"Hang on." A moment later, Trudy reappears, changed out of her work shirt and into a fresh aqua-blue blouse. She's slipped off her sneakers and now wears cute sandals.

"I'm waiting."

She sinks into one of the chairs in the waiting area. "You remember Sam Woodrich?"

"Of course I do. He was hot."

"Well, I saw Sam last night."

I dash over and sit next to her. "On a date? Tell me quick, before all your friends start pouring in, clamoring for free liquor."

"It wasn't a date, exactly."

I slap her arm. "Stop stalling."

"We ran into each other while picking up takeout and the next thing I knew, we . . . ." She pauses and glances around, as if to see who's listening.

"Had sex?" I blurt out.

"No! We had a picnic out by the lighthouse."

"That's so romantic. He always had a thing for you in high school."

"Why did everyone know that but me?"

"Because you were blinded—"

"By Larry. I know."

I get up to open some wine. "I'm so glad you didn't marry that loser."

"Would you pour me a glass, too?" Trudy rises and props open her shop door.

"White, red, or rosé?"

"White."

I pop the cork on the white, fill two plastic glasses, and give her one.

"Sam bought French pinot blanc for us to have with our dinners last night. He knows everything there is about winemaking. That's what he's been doing out in California all these years. Now he's doing consulting work for Maryland vineyards."

I can't help but titter. Maybe my sister will finally fall in love, but I know if I mention anything, she'll run like a nervous hen.

"What?" she asks.

"I think you really like this guy."

"Maybe, but you know me, Kate. I don't get too involved."

"How'd he look? Has he held up?"

Trudy's eyes sparkle. "He's heavenly. Sadly, I don't think he'll need my barbering services."

"He's bald?"

"No! He has very nice hair that he pulls back in a ponytail." She sits and spins around in her barber chair.

I haven't seen my sister like this . . . ever. I decide to forget my worries about my weight and down a piece of cheese. "Mmm."

"You'll see. That is, if he shows up."

"You invited him tonight?"

"He said he wanted to see me again. I thought this was safe enough."

I grab hold of the chair so she'll stop twirling around. "What the hell are you so afraid of, Trudy? Not all men are like my Brad, or the Neanderthal you almost married, or Dad."

"Dad?" Trudy honestly hadn't put two and two together.

Our father left our mother when I was ten and Trudy was twelve. He never missed any important events. He and Mom managed a civil relationship with one another, and after they both remarried, things settled down, but it still took its toll, especially on Trudy.

"Do you suppose that's why I've never trusted a man?" my

clueless sister asks.

"He was a wonderful father but a lousy husband." I give her chair a spin.

"Yes, I suppose he was." She stops the turning with her foot. "But Mom wasn't exactly easy."

"It takes two." Since I'm staying overnight with Kate, I meander over to top off my wine.

"What about you and Brad?" Trudy asks. "I thought things were fine. You certainly did everything you could for him, so why did this happen? It makes no sense to me."

"At first, I kept asking myself that question, but it only depressed me because I thought it was my fault. So now I try not to focus too much on 'why.' There are no clear answers, but I'm beginning to understand that the children kept us together." I giggle. "Maybe it's why we had so many, but we didn't know what to do after they were grown and out of the house."

Trudy shakes her head.

I can read her mind, so I say, "There are no guarantees, my dear sister. You just have to jump in and hope for the best."

"So why aren't *you* jumping?" she asks.

"I honestly don't know what you're talking about."

"Mrs. Lovett! Why would you back out now?"

I mull it over for a second. "I just don't want to make a fool of myself."

"Get some backbone, little sister."

Friends and neighbors begin wandering in, and as Trudy greets everyone, I pour wine for them. There are about eight people hanging out in the shop when Sam comes through the door looking like one of those gorgeous over-50 male models who are all over the Internet.

I sidle up to Trudy. "If you don't want him, I do."

"Shut up."

He's wearing jeans and a light-gray T-shirt, and carrying a plate covered with plastic wrap. He spots us and walks over.

"You didn't need to bring anything." Trudy is glowing.

I take the dish and see that it's close to overflowing with cookies that have chocolate chips, peanut butter chips, and flakes of coconut poking out the top. "On the other hand . . . these cookies could cause an orgasm."

Sam laughs. "Good to see you, Kate."

He has smoky-gray eyes and smells like fresh-cut lemons and limes.

"Wow." That's all I can say.

Trudy stares at me like she wants to kick my shins.

So I ask, "Did you make these cookies?"

"They're peanut butter chocolate cocomacs. It's my own special recipe." He winks at Trudy before hugging her, and she no longer seems to want to inflict bodily harm on me.

"Excuse me a moment." I take the plate of cookies to offer to the guests but keep close to Sam and my sister so I can listen in on their conversation.

Sam looks around the shop. "This is a great old building. I love how you've dressed the front windows with lights and antiques." He sits in one of the comfy waiting chairs. "It's all so welcoming; I might have to let you cut my hair."

"Don't you dare," my sister exclaims. She really does dig his long hair. She picks up a plastic wine glass. "I'm afraid this stuff isn't up to your standards, but would you like some?"

"Whatever's open is fine."

"Hey, aren't you Sam Woodrich?" I hear an old classmate say behind me.

After the men shake hands, Trudy gives Sam his wine and lets the men catch up. I take this opportunity and step over to my sister with the empty plate.

"Vultures." She looks at me. "Did you eat one?"

"No. I have to lose a few pounds."

"I know. You said. Do you want more wine?" Trudy asks.

I glance over to where Sam is now telling a circle of folks, who remember him, about his career in the wine business. "Nope. I want to be able to drive back to Chestertown in case my big sister gets lucky."

"No way! This is our sister night. I bought eggs and bacon to fix you breakfast."

"Okay to the eggs, but no bacon."

"So you'll stay?"

"Only if things aren't getting hot." I fan myself with my hand.

"You're incorrigible."

I pull her back to a quiet corner of the shop. "Listen to me, Trudy. I can see that you're very attracted to one another, but I'm picking up another vibe. You could have something serious here."

"I don't do serious."

"Maybe it's time you do."

My sister sighs. "I'm not up for the heartache."

"It's not going to kill you. Look at me. I'm still alive, and I wouldn't trade anything I had with Brad. We were in love for many years. And I have four beautiful children."

"Too late for that, thank God."

"Yes, it is. But there's more to marriage—"

"Marriage?" Trudy's voice is so loud that we both peer around to see if anyone, especially Sam, has overheard her. Everyone is busy with their own conversations.

I slap her arm. "Pay attention to me."

"Stop hitting me. I wanted to kick you a few minutes ago, but I held back."

"It's time to stop holding back, Trudy."

She jerks her foot back in a mock attempt to give me a good whack.

"Stop goofing around. I'm serious."

"Okay."

"I hate to see you go through life without ever knowing what it's like to be in love and to feel vulnerable." I touch her hand. "It's frightening, but it's worth it, even the painful part. It's how you know you're really alive."

"You don't mind pushing me into making a fool of myself, but you're too chicken to go back on stage."

"Okay. I may regret this, but I'll do Mrs. Lovett."

"Good." Trudy kisses my cheek. "There's something heart-warming about you giving me advice. Here I am inviting you down for the night to try to support you, but you are being the wise one. My little sister has really grown up." She laughs. "It's about time I realize you have since we're both in our sixties."

"Barely, on my count."

"But you are." Trudy smirks.

"I know."

The enticing citrus scent floats up, and we realize that Sam is standing next to us. "Thank you for inviting me."

"Are you leaving?" Trudy looks disappointed.

"I'm sorry to say that I do have to go. I have an early morning meeting with the family that is hiring me to help them with their startup. Sunday is the only day their one son can join us. He's going to have to make a career change in order for them to pull off this vineyard, so he's doing some soul-searching."

"You sound more like a counselor than a vineyard consultant," I say.

"Sometimes I am. I had a great time this evening. It gave me a chance to start reconnecting with people from home, and it was nice to see you, Kate."

"I'm glad you came by."

"I'll get your plate." Trudy starts to move, and he takes her hand.

"I'll get it later. Will you walk with me out to my car?"

"Sure." My sister lets him guide her out the door as if she might just walk anywhere he wanted to go.

I nonchalantly stand near the window and watch. Sam's Jeep is right out front, and he stops next to it. How he managed landing that parking spot is miraculous, but I get the feeling the Red Sea would part for him. He says something to Trudy. It's infuriating that I can't hear what he said. Trudy nods. He says something else. She nods again.

"Why isn't she speaking?" someone asks.

I realize that all her friends are lined up at the window, trying to catch what's happening, along with me.

Sam smiles. My sister's face is positively beaming. "I think that's a good sign," I say out loud.

"I hope so," a man behind me chimes in.

Sam kisses Trudy.

"Oh, that's an even better sign," another voice states. Several people giggle.

When he releases her and says something, she nods.

"Cat's sure got her tongue," a woman standing to my left says.

Sam gets into his Jeep and pulls away. Trudy turns and sees us all gawking at her. I smile and give her the thumbs-up. The rest of her friends in the Cambridge Creek Barbershop applaud and cheer. Clearly, she's outnumbered on this.

As Trudy comes back into the shop, I give her a bear hug before she can throttle me. "I'm so proud of you."

"Hey, you can't be the only one taking leaps of faith around here," she says.

I laugh. "I'm leaping back on stage, and you're leaping into Sam's arms."

Trudy searches my eyes. "Reassure me that you and I aren't too old for these shenanigans."

"Speak for yourself." I primp my hair and go to get more wine.

PEACEMAKER PUPPY

BEN PULLED INTO THE driveway of his new home in the Pinehurst neighborhood of Salisbury, Maryland, while his son, who was bludgeoning his way into adolescence, groaned, sliding deeper into the back seat of the SUV. Ben resisted the urge to lash out. He tried to see things from his son's point of view. Except for visits to his grandparents on the Eastern Shore, Elijah had spent his twelve years in Manhattan. In myriad ways, he made his displeasure about their move to the "boonies" perfectly clear. Ben did understand how this uprooting was adding to his son's angry attitude, but he had hopes Elijah would eventually come around.

Ben's daughter, on the other hand, threw her arms around her father's neck from her perch behind him and squealed with delight.

"Cool! The yard is huge. I love all the trees." She bounded from the car and twirled around on the front lawn with her graceful arms outstretched. Sylvia was so much like her mother once was that Ben had to wipe his eyes before opening his car door.

"Come on, buddy." Ben stepped out and stretched.

Elijah didn't respond or move. Ben left him alone. Eventually the boy's natural curiosity would win out and he'd stroll into their new house, even if it would only be to criticize everything with a scowl on his face.

"Oh, Daddy!" Sylvia had already circled the entire house at top speed. "The backyard is even bigger. It's perfect for a puppy!"

"Don't you think we have enough going on right now?" Ben knelt and hugged his nine-year-old. "Would you like to see inside?"

"Yes."

Her uneven, dark-brown braid bobbed ahead of him up to the door. Today of all days, Sylvia had asked him to try a French braid on one side like Elsa from *Frozen*. Why couldn't she have asked for Moana's or Tiana's hairstyle? Those were more easily managed with her mane of tight curls. Sylvia had her mother's hair, although Evie had always kept her own hair very short. But moving day was very special, so Ben did the best he could with the braid. After a year, he still felt like he was all thumbs when it came to his daughter's hair.

Ben fished the key out of his trouser pocket. Compared to the apartment they'd had in New York City, this three-story colonial would seem massive.

"Hurry, I can't wait to see my room." Sylvia hopped up and down on the front stoop of the white clapboard house, and as soon as Ben opened the door, she dashed up the stairs.

Ben walked into the empty formal dining room. That would be the first furniture he'd have to purchase without Evie. He couldn't imagine how to begin, but as difficult as it felt, Ben knew it was time to try to reconnect with people. He looked forward to entertaining neighbors and colleagues from his new teaching position at Salisbury University in this dining room. The outside deck was perfect for summer meals, and the children and their new friends could run around in the big yard to their hearts' content.

"This place is big enough to be a funeral home." Elijah's voice startled Ben out of his thoughts. His son stood just inside the front door.

Ben bristled at the funeral home comment. He took a deep breath. "Why don't you go check out your new room upstairs? I'm going to start unpacking the kitchen boxes so we can eat tonight."

The kitchen gleamed with stainless steel appliances put in by the seller's adult children before placing the house on the market. But there weren't any packing boxes stacked anywhere. What had happened to their dishes, utensils, pots, and pans? Ben pulled open the refrigerator door. It was stocked with essentials. His parents must have gone shopping for him. He strode over and yanked at a cabinet door. All the dishes were stacked and organized. A drawer near the sink was filled with spoons, knives, and forks. His mom and dad had unpacked his entire kitchen. His chest filled with emotion.

Because Ben had been tied up closing on their apartment, wrapping up everything at his previous teaching position, and preparing his children for the move, his parents had offered to come over from Chincoteague to meet the movers and to make sure everything was put in the proper room, but this was much more than he had expected. Ben was deeply grateful to his folks for all they continually did for him and for everything they did when Evie was sick. He and his brothers were lucky men. How his mom had survived raising them was a mystery, but she never lost her sense of humor. Thankfully, his mom and dad were now close by, and the kids could visit and go to the beach. Ben hoped that would take some of the sting out of his son's pain of giving up living in the world's greatest city.

"Dad!" Elijah shouted down the stairs. "Sylvia is in the wrong room. She took my room."

"No, I'm not." Sylvia's voice sounded tearful.

"Damn," Ben whispered and dashed up the steps to mediate.

After spending a couple of days getting nearly everything unpacked and arranged in the bedrooms and baths, Ben was finally able to set up his at-home office in the enclosed porch off the living room. Through the opened windows, he was relieved to hear his son and daughter playing with Jason, an eleven-year-old boy they had met from down the street. They sounded like they were getting along, and Ben allowed himself to concentrate on the business at hand. As he unpacked files and folders, he double-checked for anything he might need to take to his new office on campus at the Department of Communications. Ben came across his well-worn copy of Salvador Minuchin's *Families and Family Therapy.* He put it in the pile for his campus office. He would be teaching Family Communications the first semester, and it might come in handy.

"Don't you children come into my yard. You're going to trample my flowers," an unfamiliar voice shouted.

Ben looked out the window. His two children and their new friend scampered with a ball into his backyard, while a woman, with her silver hair pulled up like Katharine Hepburn's in *On Golden Pond,* stood at the property line. She wore trousers and a man's shirt, much the same as Kate often did.

Ben opened the window screen and leaned out. He extended his hand, hoping she'd walk over to shake it. "Good Morning. I'm Ben."

"I know who you are, Professor Cooper. Or should I call you 'doctor?'"

"Ben. Call me Ben." She didn't move any closer, so he lowered his hand. "We just moved in."

"I know that. What do you think I am, stupid?"

"Of course not. I was trying to make conversation."

"Whose children are they?" She seemed to eye Sylvia and Elijah in particular.

"The boy in the red shirt is from down the street. Sylvia and Elijah are mine."

The woman squinted as though the children were far away. "You adopt them?"

Ben felt his chest tighten. "No."

He didn't feel obliged to explain that his wife, who had died, was African-American, so he left it alone for now.

"Well, teach your children that it's not polite to run into other people's yards without permission." Only her mouth moved when she spoke. The rest of her body was motionless.

"I guess they were going after their ball."

"They didn't ask if they could get it." She continued her statue-like appearance.

"I'm sorry. Would it be okay if one of them came over to retrieve the ball if it rolls into your yard?"

"They have to ask."

"Oh. I see. I'll speak to them about it."

"See that you do." She finally shifted and marched back into her brick house.

Ben didn't lower his head far enough and banged it on the window sash. He rubbed the sore spot and muttered, "That's what I call real Southern hospitality." When he looked back over at her house, he caught her peering out in his direction. He started to smile, but her curtains snapped shut. "This may not be as easy as I'd hoped."

The window air conditioner whined as Ben and his children ate the leftover meatloaf, mashed potatoes, and string beans he had cooked the night before when it was cooler.

"I'm going to be a dancer like Mommy was." Sylvia cut a string bean into small pieces.

"You can be whatever you want." Ben turned to his son. "Jason seems cool."

Elijah shrugged. "He's okay."

"The lady next door was upset today."

"We didn't do anything." Elijah quickly defended himself.

"I'm sure you didn't intend to, but she'd like you to ask permission before going into her yard next time."

Elijah rolled his eyes and forked up a blob of mashed potatoes.

"I'm afraid things could be different here. We aren't in Manhattan."

Ben's son swallowed and said, "You're not kidding. Why did we have to move here?"

Because I can't live in the apartment without your mother. Because I need to be near my parents. Because I must find a way to start over. Ben found his voice. "So we can be closer to the beach."

Right on cue, his angelic daughter changed the topic.

"Jason volunteers with his mom at the animal shelter," Sylvia said casually, as she ate a morsel of her beans.

"It's called the Humane Society, stupid."

"Don't be rude to your sister."

"Jason said they have lots of dogs up for adoption." Sylvia glanced at her brother before taking a bite of mashed potatoes.

Afraid of making matters worse by directly shooting down the idea of getting a dog, Ben only nodded. He knew that while Sylvia would like a puppy, she was angling for her brother, who desperately wanted one. Elijah didn't know it, but he had a gem of a sister. Hopefully that would get through his thick head at some point.

"Can we go to the beach soon?" Elijah asked, before downing more meatloaf. There was nothing wrong with his appetite.

Ben was relieved Elijah had shifted the topic off dogs, because right now, he just couldn't face the work a puppy required.

"I hope so, but the people are coming to put in the central air conditioning. These old-fashioned window units are too noisy, and they do nothing for this stickiness." Ben pulled at his T-shirt before drinking some iced tea. "We'll have to be here while it's being installed."

"Grammy and Pop Pop won't mind watching us," Sylvia chimed in. "They said so."

"I know. We'll see how things go. But I'll make sure we go soon."

"Can I be excused?" Elijah set down his fork.

"May I."

"May I be excused? Jason wants me to help him with his pitching after dinner."

Ben usually asked Elijah to wait until everyone was done with dinner, but if he was making a friend, maybe he'd be happier. "After you rinse your plate and utensils and set them in the dishwasher."

"May I go, too?" Sylvia ate her first piece of meatloaf.

Elijah opened his mouth, but before he could complain, Ben waved him away from the table. "Sylvia, why don't we spend some time hanging those pictures you wanted on the walls of your room?"

"Okay."

"But eat some more first."

Once Elijah had loaded his dinner plate into the dishwasher, he grabbed his baseball and mitt from the bench in the mudroom and slammed out the back door.

"In before dark," Ben hollered. It was different being back on the Eastern Shore. He'd be able to give Elijah more independence. Maybe that would be a plus across from the negatives on his son's mental list about moving here.

"Do you still miss Mommy?" Sylvia's sweet voice cut through

the armor Ben tried to hold up around his children. They needed to know he was in control and everything was okay.

"Yes, honey, I do. Very much. How about you?"

She nodded while swirling her fork in her mashed potatoes.

Ben had wanted to move immediately after Evie's death, but the grief counselor suggested waiting a year. It would be better for the children to stay in their home and return to their schools and see their friends. Ben had a teaching contract to fulfill for a year anyway, but he did begin job and house hunting in areas where he'd grown up and where his parents still lived.

"Do you want to talk about it?" Ben asked.

"I heard Elijah crying last night."

"Oh. Do you think it was about moving or about Mommy?"

"He misses her, but he won't admit it. I think it's why he's still so sad and seems mad a lot."

"You're very observant, Sylvia. The thing is that everyone handles loss in different ways. Elijah has to figure this out his way, and you can do it your way."

"Okay." His daughter went back to eating. "You make really good meatloaf, Daddy."

When Ben answered the door, Jason bolted in. "Hi, Ben. This is my mom."

"Jason! You will address your friend's father as mister." She put out her hand. "I'm sorry; Jason hasn't told me your last name."

"Cooper." Ben shook her hand. "But I told him he could call me Ben."

"Jason?" His mother was obviously in control of her son.

"Sorry, Mr. Cooper."

Ben ruffled the boy's hair. "That's fine. Elijah and Sylvia are up in their rooms. You can go on up."

The boy dashed up the stairs.

"I'm a single mom, and I need to use a firm hand. Jason's father is very involved with him, which is a blessing, but he lives in DC."

"I understand. Won't you come in?" Ben led Jason's mother to the living room. "What is your name?"

Ben found it endearing that her cheeks turn rosy. "Oh, I was so shocked when Jason called you by your first name that I forgot to introduce myself. I'm Devyn Farrell-Smith." She shook his hand again with a firm grip. Her skin was soft. "Welcome to the neighborhood."

"Thank you." Ben noticed Devyn admiring the duck carving on the mantel.

She walked closer to the fireplace. "What a beautiful pintail drake."

"My father gave it to me. It had been his dad's. We're a family of birders."

"I assume you've been to the Ward Museum of Wildfowl Art here in Salisbury?"

"I have, but not for a long time. I'm looking forward to taking my son and daughter."

"Jason and I enjoy going there."

"Please sit down." Ben gestured.

Devyn sat on the couch.

"Can I get you some iced tea?"

"No, thank you."

Ben sat across from her. "I understand what you were saying before about being a single parent. It's been a year since my wife died, and I'm still trying to figure it all out."

"I'm sorry. I didn't know."

"I guess Elijah didn't say anything to Jason. He's very quiet about it."

"He just mentioned you. I didn't know if you were married or not."

Sylvia dashed into the living room. "Hi, I'm Sylvia." She leaned over the arm of the sofa.

"Nice to meet you. I'm Ms. Farrell-Smith." She smiled at Ben's daughter. "How old are you?"

"I'm nine."

"Would you like to sit next to me?"

Sylvia slipped in next to the woman. "I like your haircut."

Devyn ran one hand through her short, red hair. "It's easy."

"Daddy and I have problems with my hair. Mommy used to do it."

"I like all your curls."

"I have Mommy's hair, don't I, Daddy?"

"Yes, you do, sweetheart."

Devyn looked at Ben. "And you have your Daddy's green eyes."

Sylvia leapt up. "I'll show you a picture of Mommy on stage." She raced into her father's office.

Ben held Devyn's gaze. "Until she became sick, Evie danced with the Alvin Ailey American Dance Theatre."

Sylvia returned, carrying a framed photograph.

Devyn looked at the picture of the famous African-American dance company. A striking woman in a sky-blue leotard had been captured mid-leap. "She's beautiful, Sylvia. I'm sorry she died."

Ben was touched by Devyn's sincere nature and how comfortable she was with his daughter.

"She couldn't get better, so she became an angel." Sylvia put the photograph on the table. "Daddy, can we go with Ms. Farrell-Smith and the boys to the animal shelter today?"

Devyn looked at Ben. "Could you? That would be fun."

Ben didn't answer right away.

"You probably have other plans."

"Can we?"

"Would you put Mommy's picture back in my office for me, dear?"

"Yep." Sylvia gently picked up the framed photograph and carried it away.

"Ben, I'm sorry. I should have waited until you answered for yourself. Jason had invited Elijah so he could show him where he volunteers with me. I don't want Sylvia to be disappointed now." Devyn toyed with a necklace around her neck.

"The kids want a dog, and I'm afraid that if we go and see all those poor homeless pups, we'll—"

"Bring one home?"

"Exactly, but I have a lot on my plate right now." Ben shook his head. "I know the kids want one, especially Elijah. He was enamored with our neighbor's dog in Manhattan."

"I understand. No one should get a dog unless they're ready."

"But I'll take my chances. If my son is going with you today, it's only fair that Sylvia gets to go, too."

As they were all loading into Devyn's SUV in Ben's driveway, Jason said, "Mom, your new dress for Chelsea's wedding is back here."

"Oh, I forgot to carry that into the house. It's for my niece's wedding."

Jason held the long plastic bag by the hanger. "Do you want

me to run it home?"

"I'll just put it in my house," said Ben, taking the bag from Jason. "You can pick it up when we get back."

As Ben jogged back to his front door, Devyn called out, "Thank you."

After Ben returned and got in and the children were settled in the back seat, Devyn backed out of the driveway. "Half the time I'm driving around Jason's soccer team or little league team, so I need this monster vehicle. It does come in handy."

"Mom, may we watch a video back here?"

"Yes. But you have to agree on one and no arguing with your guests."

The kids became involved with their own conversation, and Ben settled back in his seat. "I'm grateful that my children met your son."

"Me, too. When school starts, they can all walk together since it's only a few blocks away."

"And if they need me, I'll be close by at Salisbury University. I start teaching in the Communications Department this fall. I'm concerned about having uprooted them, but I felt it was time to move back to the Eastern Shore."

"You grew up here?" Devyn steered onto Snow Hill Road.

"Yes, my folks are on Chincoteague Island. Since I'm raising the kids alone now, I wanted to be closer to my parents. They are very happy about it. Elijah and Sylvia love them, and the kids are crazy about the beach."

"I'm sure they'll enjoy seeing their grandchildren more often."

"Yes, and although Mom and Dad are both healthy, it's not a bad idea to be nearby in case they need me, too."

"I grew up in Easton. Moved here when Jay and I got married. The house is too big for just the two of us now, but Jay and I didn't want to disrupt our son any more than necessary.

Luckily, between my salary and the child support, Jason and I can stay put."

"It's good that you and Jay have put your son first."

"Thanks for saying so. Like all divorces, it's complicated, but we do our best."

"So it sounds like you work. What do you do?"

"I'm a veterinarian."

"Oh, so when you volunteer at the Humane Society, you're. . . . "

"Taking care of the animals. We examine them. Sometimes they need medicine or surgery."

"Wow. That's wonderful."

"Thanks. It's why Jason can volunteer. Volunteers have to be over eighteen, but I'm there whenever he's helping." Devyn made a left onto Airport Road.

Ben turned to his children. "You need to address Jason's mom as Dr. Farrell-Smith."

"Okay." Elijah went back to watching the video.

"Understand, Sylvia?"

His daughter's confused expression broke Ben's heart. "What kind of doctor is she? Like you, Daddy, or like Mommy's doctors?"

Ben reached back to pat her knee. "Neither. She's a vet. She's a doctor for animals."

Sylvia relaxed. "Cool."

Devyn smiled. "Jason should refer to you as Dr. Cooper, then."

"I'm not that formal about it." Ben laughed. "I'm fine with Ben, remember?"

"Yes, I do." Devyn glanced at Ben. "Is your doctorate in communications?"

"I have one in Communication Sciences and one in Family Studies."

"You and your wife were both high achievers."

"Yes, I guess so."

Devyn pulled into the parking lot. "We're here."

They got out of the car, entered the building, and walked along the row of cages. Devyn and her son told Ben and his children what was known about each dog. Some of the dogs clamored for attention while others cowered in the corner.

"It's so sad. I want to take them all home." Sylvia lingered at every cage.

Ben wondered if this had been a good idea. Elijah seemed to be handling things better than his sister until they reached a Chesapeake Bay retriever with big brown eyes.

"Oh, Daddy." Elijah squatted in front of the crate. The puppy wagged its tail.

His son hadn't called him that in some time, and Ben knew he was in trouble.

"This good boy was tearfully given up by a recent college graduate who couldn't take the dog home to New England," Devyn explained. "He's a year old, in perfect health, and house-trained."

"What's more perfect than a Chesapeake Bay retriever since we're living here now, Dad?" Elijah stared at the dog.

Sylvia went down on the floor next to her brother and peered into the cage at the puppy, who seemed to know he'd just found his new best friends.

Sylvia stood with her father on the deck, watching her brother run in the backyard with the puppy. "We should let Elijah name him."

Ben hugged his girl. She was wise beyond her years. "Yes, we will do that."

The puppy's paws were still too big for his body, but he managed to keep ahead of Elijah and bolted toward the neighbor's yard.

"Damn," Ben whispered. "Elijah, let me handle this." Ben chased after the dog. "Come! Come back, dog."

Ben's unfriendly neighbor flew out of her back door. "Stop!"

The puppy skidded to a halt, and Ben took hold of his collar. "I'm sorry about this. We just brought him home, and he's a little rambunctious."

"That dog can't just run into my garden like that." Her hands were on her hips, but she still controlled her movement.

"I'll make sure it doesn't happen again, Mrs. . . . I don't know your name." The dog tugged Ben away a few steps. "We're neighbors, and I'd like to know your name."

"It's Mrs. Spence. Keep that dog and your children away from my property." She stormed back into her house.

"Holy moly." Ben wasn't used to people reacting to him or his children this way. He'd always prided himself on getting along with folks, and he'd taught his children to be polite and gracious to others. Ben didn't like to assume this woman was a bigot, but she wouldn't be the first one he had encountered. He hoped she just wanted to be left alone and wouldn't say nasty things to his children.

Elijah and his sister stood at the edge of their yard. Elijah had retrieved the dog leash the Humane Society had sent home with them.

"Clip the leash on him." Ben tried to hold the wiggling dog still.

"I'm sorry, Dad." Elijah, who hadn't been very contrite lately, was obviously motivated to keep the dog. "He just got away from me."

"It's not your fault. You need to name the dog, teach him his name, and work on commands like 'come.' You must keep him on a leash in the yard. We can get a longer one so he can burn off some of this energy, and we'll find a dog park where he can run loose. Let's go inside and make a list of everything we need to buy for this little guy."

"Thanks, Dad."

"It will all work out, son. Dogs are a lot of work and responsibility."

"I understand. I'll take good care of Boomer."

"Boomer?" Sylvia wrinkled her nose but didn't argue.

Ben laughed. "That's the perfect name for this ball of fire."

"So, what's the story with our neighbor?" Ben asked when he phoned Devyn to get the okay for Jason to stay overnight.

Devyn paused.

"Please tell me I haven't moved next door to an ax murderer."

"Nothing like that. Honestly, I'm not sure how to answer. If I lived next door to her, maybe I could tell you more. But since we're down the street, I don't know her. She was very close with the woman who owned your house. I saw them together a lot."

"My real estate agent told me the woman didn't want to leave her home, but she wasn't well enough to stay alone. She was moving into an 'in-law suite' at her son's home in Florida. Maybe Mrs. Spence misses her friend. I hope that's it." Ben hesitated to share his deeper concerns about his next-door neighbor. "I'm not sure how to win her over, and I'm usually pretty good at that."

Devyn laughed. "Yes, you are."

"Have I won you over, Dr. Farrell-Smith?"

"Time will tell."

Ben caught sight of Boomer racing toward the house with

something unfamiliar in his mouth, followed by his unhappy neighbor. "Oh, boy. I'm afraid I have to go. My dog is in trouble with Mrs. Spence again."

"Good luck."

"Thanks."

The front doorbell rang, and if it could have an angry tone, it did.

Ben wondered where the children were as he zipped to the front door and opened it.

"Your dog has stolen my gardening hat." On the jog over, wisps of Mrs. Spence's hair had loosened from her bun.

"Good afternoon, Mrs. Spence."

Ben noticed that she was trying to peek around him to see inside. "Would you like to come in?"

She stood like a statue again. "No. I want my hat."

Sylvia arrived next to her father, hiding the hat behind her back. "I'm sorry Boomer got into your yard again. He pulled too hard, and I let go of the leash so he didn't drag me into your yard along with him."

Ben was relieved to notice Mrs. Spence fighting a smile. He wanted to say that her face wouldn't crack, but he thought he might be pushing things.

"I'm Sylvia." She produced the hat. "Here's your hat. I don't think Boomer hurt it." She brushed a leaf off the brim.

Mrs. Spence snatched her hat away. "Keep that dog out of my garden." She spun around so quickly, she nearly missed the next step.

Ben reached out to catch her, but she righted herself and strode across to her house.

Sylvia shut the door. "Why is she so mean?"

Ben put his hand on her shoulder. "I don't know, but we'll find out. Try not to let her upset you. It's her problem, not yours."

"Can we help her?"

"I hope so. Where are your brother and Jason?"

"Out back. They're afraid you're going to be angry."

This was too much additional stress on his children. That woman had to be reached, but how?

The children worked with Boomer to come when they called him and to go in and out of his new crate, which was located in a corner of the family room. Luckily, the dog had been house-trained by his previous owner, but in all other ways, Boomer was an untrained puppy. He wanted to jump up on people. He thought he could hop up on the sofa. He tried to chew everything except the ten toys they'd bought. But when the dog was affectionate, and Ben saw the look on his children's faces, he knew he'd made the right decision. Maybe he'd look online for a dog training class nearby. He'd just sat down at his laptop when Sylvia came in, out of breath, holding an unfamiliar gardening glove.

"Don't tell me." Ben looked out his office window, but he didn't see Mrs. Spence. "What happened?"

"Daddy, I need to tell you something." Boomer collapsed flat on the rug next to Sylvia with his tongue hanging out of his mouth.

"Did that dog steal Mrs. Spence's glove?"

Sylvia's eyes wandered toward the window.

"Why isn't she coming over here to yell at us?" Ben asked.

"Because she gave it to Boomer." Sylvia looked back at her father. "I opened the back door, and Boomer scooted out before I could stop him. I told him to come, but he ran right over to Mrs. Spence's back door. I followed him this time, but she didn't see me because I got nervous and hid behind the bushes. She petted him and talked to him. Boomer's tail was going a mile a minute."

"Really?" Ben was astonished.

"Then she tossed her glove on the ground and told him to 'leave it.' And he did. I think there's something about her voice that makes him listen to her."

"He doesn't listen to any of us very well."

"She had a box of treats on the back step, and when he behaved, she gave him one. Then she picked up the glove, tossed it again, and told him to 'get it.' When he picked it up, she said, 'take it.' She pointed at our house, and he ran home. I was so surprised that I forgot I was hiding. I stood right up. When she saw me, I thought she was going to yell at me. Her mouth opened, but then she sort of freaked. She grabbed her treat box and ran inside."

"I see."

"You do? Because I don't understand. Why would she want Boomer to take her glove? Why isn't she over here yelling at us?"

Ben laughed. "You have solved it, Sylvia!"

Boomer wagged his tail.

"I did?"

"Mrs. Spence wants an excuse to come over here."

Sylvia pondered for a moment. "Is she lonely?"

"Yes, I think she is. But when she knew that you discovered her plan, she was embarrassed."

"I ruined it."

"No. Not at all. If we didn't know the truth, we would still be stumped. But now we can make a plan. Please ask your brother to come in here." While Sylvia scooted upstairs, Ben texted a message to Devyn, who was at work.

"Barbeque tomorrow night here. You and J.? Mrs. S. invited."

"Interesting. Wouldn't miss it. Will bring three-bean salad."

"BTW your dress for your niece's wedding is still hanging in my hall closet."

"Sorry. Will take it home after barbeque."

"Seems like you don't want to go."

"Not without a date."

Ben smiled. "I might be able to do something about that."

"But why do I have to go talk to her?" Elijah was having difficulty following the plan. "Sylvia is the one who let the dog run out the door."

"I don't mind going," Sylvia chimed in.

Ben smirked. His daughter was fearless. "Elijah, what are you going to say when you go up to her front door?"

"I'm going to apologize for the dog stealing her glove and invite her to the barbeque."

"Exactly. Sylvia can't go over because she knows the truth. We need to help Mrs. Spence save face." Ben handed the glove to his son.

"Okay. I get it." Elijah started for the door. Ben and Sylvia watched Elijah through the office window. He walked up to Mrs. Spence's front door and rang the bell. He talked briefly with the neighbor, sprinted off her porch, and when he was clear of her yard, he gave his father and sister the thumbs-up.

"She's coming!" Sylvia threw her arms up in the air.

Mrs. Spence arrived in the backyard, carrying what smelled like freshly baked brownies.

"Welcome, Mrs. Spence." Ben was flipping hamburgers on the grill.

"Hi, I'm Devyn from down the street, and this is my son, Jason."

All three children held back uncertainly while Mrs. Spence stared at them. Boomer pulled away from Elijah and jumped up on the guest.

While holding her brownies aloft, Mrs. Spence said, "Down." Boomer immediately put all four feet on the ground.

"Can you teach me how to make him do that?" Elijah asked.

Mrs. Spence handed her plate of brownies to Devyn and pulled a dog yummy out of her pocket. "Sit." The dog sat.

Everyone laughed.

"How do you know how to make him listen?" Sylvia asked.

"I was a professional dog trainer."

"Wow," Elijah said.

"These burgers are just about ready." Ben spoke to his son. "Would you get Mrs. Spence something to drink?"

Elijah nodded. "Mrs. Spence, would you like some iced tea or lemonade?"

"Iced tea would be nice. Thank you."

"Do you want to sit next to me?" Sylvia asked the neighbor. "I promise not to spill anything on you."

"Okay." There was a tiny smile on Mrs. Spence's face.

After everyone claimed their spots, Ben brought the burgers to the table and the food and condiments were passed around. Sylvia couldn't get the ketchup bottle opened, and before Ben could help her, Devyn took care of it.

"Thank you for bringing the brownies." Ben poured more juice into Jason's glass.

"Homemade." Mrs. Spence took a helping of three-bean salad.

"I'm looking forward to sampling them, but you didn't have to bring anything but yourself."

"I enjoy baking. Your invitation gave me a reason to do it again." She ate a forkful of salad. "This three-bean salad is delicious."

"Dr. Farrell-Smith made it." Sylvia took a spoonful from the bowl for her plate.

Devyn's eyes met Mrs. Spence's. "I'm a veterinarian, but please call me Devyn."

"Are you the reason they got this dog?" Mrs. Spence asked.

Ben wasn't sure if she was blaming Devyn or just asking an innocent question. "We got him at the Humane Society where Devyn does volunteer veterinarian work."

"Good place. I'm a member." Mrs. Spence bit into her burger. "Nice job with the grill, Dr. Cooper."

"Thanks. Call me Ben."

Sylvia pushed at a slice of pickle with her fork. "I'm sorry your friend had to leave this house, Mrs. Spence. You must miss her."

Mrs. Spence stopped chewing. Everyone else held their breath, waiting to see how she would react.

"I do miss her. We met back in 1970 when we both moved into these houses with our husbands and children. Linda and I had so much in common that we immediately became best friends. We were there for each other through the good times and the bad. Our children grew up and moved away. Our husbands died. But we still had each other . . . until now."

"Could you fly down to visit her?" Devyn asked. "I'd be happy to take you to the airport."

"Thank you. I plan to go over the holidays. Her son has been kind enough to include me."

"That'll be nice." Ben grabbed his napkin away from Boomer, who was skulking around the table, hoping for a treat.

"It will." Mrs. Spence appeared older and wistful. "I email long letters to her, but she's having trouble typing back because of her arthritis. It's the daily communication I miss. We were always talking. When our husbands were around, they'd joke about us never running out of conversation."

"Do you know how to FaceTime?" Elijah asked.

Mrs. Spence grimaced. "I'm lucky if I can manage an email. No, I don't."

"I'll teach you." Elijah smiled. "Then you can chat and see each other whenever you'd like."

"I'd appreciate that, young man."

"May we be excused?" Jason asked his mother.

The children had eaten all they were going to eat until brownies later.

"I'm going to ask you each to carry your dirty plates in and set them in Dr. Cooper's sink."

The children bolted, and Boomer followed them into the house.

"What can I get you, Mrs. Spence?"

"Please call me Evelyn."

"That was my wife's name. She passed away a year ago."

"I'm so sorry," Mrs. Spence said.

"She liked to be called Evie."

"Judging from your children, I'm sure she must have been a lovely person."

"Thank you. She was." Ben took a drink of his iced tea and quietly sighed a breath of relief. Maybe Mrs. Spence was okay.

"Would you like more salad, Evelyn?" Devyn asked.

"I would. It's really good."

"Anyone need another burger? I can grill more."

Devyn groaned. "Too full."

"Have to save room for dessert," Evelyn said.

The boys dashed out of the house and began chasing a ball

around in the grass with the dog.

When the adults walked into the kitchen, Sylvia was rinsing the dishes.

"Thanks." Ben kissed her head. "You can go play. I'll take care of this."

"Would you like to see the house, Mrs. Spence?" Sylvia asked. "This way, you can tell your friend what it looks like now." She took hold of the older woman's hand and led her out of the kitchen.

"Who knew?" Ben set dishes in the dishwasher.

"It's a miracle." Devyn put plastic wrap over the three-bean salad and placed it in Ben's refrigerator.

"I appreciate you and Jason joining us at the last minute. I thought it might balance things out more for Mrs. Spence."

Devyn moved to Ben at the counter. "So, is that the only reason you invited me?"

Ben closed the dishwasher. "No, it wasn't."

"Go on."

"I wanted to see you again."

"I like that reason."

"I'm glad." Ben noticed Devyn toying with her necklace again. "What is that on your necklace?"

Devyn held out the small glass ball. "There are four mustard seeds in it."

"There must be some significance to it."

Sylvia and Evelyn walked back into the kitchen just as Devyn said, "It was a gift from my ex-husband's husband."

Ben turned sharply toward his older neighbor. He hoped she wouldn't say something unkind.

"Love is love." Mrs. Spence still held Sylvia's hand.

"Jason's dad is gay. Isn't that cool?" Sylvia asked.

"Very cool." Mrs. Spence opened the back door. "We're going to play with the boys and Boomer. We can have the brownies when you're ready."

"I continue to be astonished." Ben looked out the window to see both boys rolling in the grass with Boomer. He turned back to Devyn. "So that's why your marriage ended."

"Yes. Jason's father finally came to terms with his sexual orientation and moved out. I loved him. I still do—as a friend."

"You're amazing."

"Not really. I was shocked and hurt, but there was no sense feeling hateful. Jay was always faithful to me during our marriage. He's a wonderful father. He met Tyler a few months after he moved to DC. I was a little worried when they wanted to get married so quickly, but Tyler turned out to be a great guy. He gave me this necklace to symbolize his new family. The seeds are Tyler, Jay, Jason, and me."

"Very nice."

"I have no regrets. I wouldn't have Jason if I hadn't married Jay. Tyler is like a second father to our son. It all worked out."

Ben carefully looked at her. "I may be going out on a limb, but you seem a little sad."

Devyn tucked her necklace inside her T-shirt. "I guess I want what Jay has, but I haven't even dated. I can't face that whole deal."

Ben shivered. "Me, either."

They both turned toward the window. Evelyn was coaching each of the kids to make Boomer heel next to them.

"Maybe we could help each other." Devyn's hand was on the counter next to Ben's. He let his pinky touch hers.

"How?" Devyn smiled but kept looking out the window.

"We could skip the whole dating scene and try some dates of our own."

"Do you mean you and me, Dr. Cooper?"

"Yes, if that's appealing to you, Dr. Farrell-Smith."

"It is under one condition."

Ben grinned. "Name it."

"One of our dates is my niece's upcoming wedding in Easton."

"Deal."

Devyn put her hand in his. "Maybe we can get Evelyn to sit with the kids for the day."

Elijah appeared at the door and asked, "May we have brownies now?"

Boomer bounded in and jumped up on Ben. "Maybe I can get Evelyn to train this puppy."

WATERWOMAN

A S I SLAM THE door and charge down the front steps like a truculent tween, I experience an immediate adrenaline rush, but within seconds, I feel like a jerk. God, I let my mother get under my skin something fierce. A mosquito bites my arm. I slap it dead. Blood mixes with the sweat on my skin. "Damn it." I flick the carcass onto the sidewalk and turn to go back inside. When I reach the stoop of my parents' Rock Hall bungalow, I hear Mom's voice through the living room window.

"Counting college and her first year working, Kaleigh's been gone five years, but she doesn't seem to have grown up much."

Daddy's reply is slow and deliberate. "Give her some room, Sue." He has to focus to form the words. "You've always been too hard on her."

"She's still a Daddy's girl. You're the reason she's so off-center."

I step back onto the cement and walk toward Rock Hall Harbor, hoping to find a breeze down there.

A couple of weeks ago, Mom called me while I was at work, which she'd never done. When I saw her caller ID, I knew something bad had happened. Since Dad is a waterman and makes his living on the Chesapeake Bay, we were always relieved to see him walking back up from the boat. Unless I was out there with him, which I was every chance I got once I was big enough to help, I worried. Although she tried to hide it, Mom did, too. Depending on the time of year and what he was catching, I grew up with her starting to look out for him at whatever time the season dictated his return.

My boss didn't allow personal cell phone calls during working hours, but I knew I had to answer. Without saying hello, I immediately asked, "What's wrong?"

"Your father's had a stroke."

Thank God he hadn't drowned or had an accident on the boat, but I didn't comprehend what she meant exactly. "A stroke? Is he going to be okay?"

"He's alive, but it's too soon to know how much he'll get back. Harley and Jack offloaded their catch and came in right after him. At first, those asses thought he was goofing around when he couldn't speak clearly or move his right arm or leg. When they realized he wasn't joking, they called 911 and tried to reassure him until the Kent Rescue Squad arrived." Her voice shook. "We're lucky it hit him on shore, or he might have died."

The Rock of Gibraltar wasn't her usual stoic self, and my Superman father had found his kryptonite.

"When are you supposed to be here for Chelsea's bridal shower?" she asked.

"In five days."

"I need you to come home now, Kaleigh."

I was on the first plane I could catch back to the East Coast.

As I near the harbor, I take in a deep breath, and the familiar fishy air settles me after my blow-up with Mom. It's getting close to sunset, and the white reflections of the small fleet of Chesapeake Bay deadrise workboats glisten in the water. I wander out the finger pier to the *Kaleigh Sue* and jump aboard. This isn't the first time I've escaped to Daddy's boat since my return to the Eastern Shore a couple of weeks ago. I run my fingers over the throttle, itching to take her out. That's what Mom and I argued about. She doesn't want me out on the bay by myself. I can handle it, even if I'm a little rusty. I told her it's like riding a bicycle. Once you've done it, it comes back to you. Plus, it's in my blood.

I sit on the engine box cover to watch an osprey hover above the water, eyeing the swirl of action kicked up by a school of baitfish. It swoops down, catches its dinner in its talons, and begins carrying the small, silver menhaden off to a tree. Several feet up in the air, the bird shakes the wet off its wings and body like a dog after a swim. I shake my head, wondering more and more why I ever left the bay. What was I doing in Los Angeles?

"Ooh-wee."

A voice startles me out of my thoughts.

"As I live and breathe, is that Kaleigh Strong sittin' in her daddy's deadrise?"

I turn toward the dock. Parker Watts smiles down at me. Despite his being a year behind me in school, he'd always seemed older. He was tall for his age, or maybe it was his old soul. We were friendly back in the day, and now this tall drink of water reminds me of how thirsty I am.

"Permission to come aboard, captain."

I nod.

He steps onto the deck and leans against the wheelhouse in his friendly, nonchalant manner. "Come down to watch the sunset? Going to be a pretty one."

I am unable to form words.

"Aren't you going to say anything?"

"Hey."

"Hey back. Sorry to hear about your daddy's stroke. How's he doing?"

"He's making progress."

"Will he be able to get back out there?" Parker lifts his chin toward the bay.

I shift my gaze in the same direction. The sun is dipping closer to the horizon, shooting rosy ribbons across the slate-gray water. "I doubt it, but never say never." I look at Parker. "So, what have you been up to?"

"College. Home for the summer. Looking for a job." His tan skin glows in the evening light, and strands of gold emerge in his sandy-colored hair.

"I thought you worked for your Uncle Gab during summers."

Parker is a natural waterman. When he was only thirteen, he won the docking competition during the annual Rock Hall Watermen's Appreciation Day. Single-engine boats can be buggers to operate in reverse gear. Watching him maneuver his daddy's thirty-eight-foot single-screw workboat into a slip, faster and cleaner than any of the grown men who'd worked the bay their whole lives, was a sight to see.

Parker frowns as he faces the glaring sunset. "I did. My dad's had some problems. He's working with Gab this season . . . and next."

I know I'm pushing, but this news makes me curious. "What about your father's boat?"

Sliding down the wheelhouse wall, Parker sits on the deck. "He had to sell it. It's complicated."

Watermen don't sell their boats. They are left to someone in the family and often to the next generation.

"So, your uncle can't use both of you?"

"He said he would, but I know he doesn't have the money to pay two of us. He won't let me work for free, so I'm prowling the docks, hoping to pick up something."

"I'm sorry about your father's boat. It must have broken your heart to see him lose the *Lickety Split.*"

"It put a dent in my day. I hope I can buy it back someday." Parker rests his head back on the wall of the wheelhouse. "How about you? What are you doing besides helping out your folks this summer?"

I start to neaten up a coil of line that I had already straightened the last time I was aboard. "I want to be helping them financially."

I decide not to share the embarrassing detail that if I hadn't spent this first year after college supporting my freeloading "actor" boyfriend, I'd have a little savings to offer them.

"You're working out in California, right?" Parker asks.

"I was. But Mom needs me, and I want to be here. I can't be in two places at once, and my boss said if I didn't come back after my two-week 'vacation' to help out with my father, I might as well not come back at all."

"Nice guy."

"He's a dickhead." I find a tiny pebble stuck to the bottom of my sneaker and toss it into the drink. "I'm supposed to fly back tomorrow night if I intend to keep my job."

"You're not going, are you?"

"Nope."

Parker nods his approval.

"I'm done with Los Angeles. Never intended to end up there anyway."

He scrutinizes me. "Weren't you majoring in business?"

"Yep. I'd planned to come back here and help Dad expand the business. He's one of those men who's in love with the bay, but not as great with the nuts and bolts of commerce." I lift the engine box cover and start checking the John Deere diesel engine. "He does okay. He kept food on the table and put me through school, but I always felt we could go bigger with the right know-how."

Parker lumbers up and wanders closer to look at the engine. He's clean shaven and smells like freshly washed cotton. "How did you end up in Hollywood after college?"

"A guy. Dirk. It's over."

"Is that a good thing or a bad thing?"

"Great. It's freaking great." While staring absently at the engine, I berate myself again for letting my heart and my hormones take me away from my family. Maybe Dad wouldn't have had this stroke if I'd come back last year and worked with him. "Dirk the Jerk is still in the apartment. He'd better pay the rent because I'm not anymore. Eventually, I may go out there to get some of my things, but I have no attachment to any of it."

"Welcome home, Kaleigh." Parker smiles at me, and the genuine care in his voice is a relief after the hard knocks of LA.

"It's good to be back." The sun dips into the water. "Look," I say. "She's going in."

"Good night, sun." Parker gives a wave like we often did as children. Music begins to float down the harbor from Waterman's Crab House Restaurant and Dock Bar. "Come on, Kaleigh, I'll buy you a beer to celebrate your return to the Eastern Shore."

"That's right. You're 'legal' now, aren't you?"

"Turned twenty-one last month."

I lower the engine box cover and wipe my hands on a rag. "But you don't have a job."

"Neither do you. I'll buy the first round and you can pay for the second."

I slip my phone out of my back pocket and check the time. "Hmm. I'd better go home first. Mom will need help getting Dad into bed. Maybe I'll be able to stop over later."

"Is he still going to bed early like he's getting up before dawn?"

"Once a waterman, always a waterman."

"Early to bed, unless there's some good brews to enjoy nearby."

"Right." I laugh as I hop onto the finger pier. But my waterman father doesn't drink. He gave it up when I was born, or so the story goes.

Parker smoothly steps off the boat deck and onto the pier. "Hope to see you later, Kaleigh. We do need to toast your return."

When I reach home, my parents are watching a rerun of *Modern Family*. It's good to hear Dad laugh. As I walk in, Mom gives me the cold shoulder. She'll settle down in a bit. She usually does.

At the end of the show, Dad turns the TV off. He tightens his jaw in concentration before saying, "Handy things, these remotes. I didn't appreciate them as much before now."

I make an attempt at being casual when I ask, "Do either of you know what happened to Mr. Watts? I ran into Parker Watts down at the harbor, and he told me his dad had to sell his deadrise."

My folks exchange a look before Mom whispers as if someone might be eavesdropping in our living room. "He got hooked on drugs."

Dad grunts his disapproval of her answer and slowly but firmly speaks. "He fell off his boat last year. Hit the gunwale before going into the water. Then he got hooked on the painkillers. That can happen to anyone."

For reasons beyond my understanding, Gus Watts has always been a bit of a rival of my dad's, and this was the first time I'd heard my father come to the man's defense. Maybe his stroke was softening him up.

Mom stands up. "About ready for bed, Earl?"

"Yep. I'll try to read a little in bed." Dad's always loved to read, and I'm happy to hear that he is working to get back to it. Anything that stimulates his mind might help his speech continue to improve.

We follow Dad as he shuffles down the hall with his walker to the bathroom. Mom keeps her hand outstretched toward his back as if he might fall backward at any moment. She knows better than to hold on to him. He'd bristle at that. But she needs me to help her if he does stumble. She says she can't catch him by herself. At best, we might manage to break his fall. But it's reassuring to my mother that I'm here just in case.

Daddy shuts the bathroom door behind him. "You two don't have to hover like a pair of helicopters. I'll call when I'm ready."

"Be sure you do." Mom steps into their room and sits on the foot of their bed. I hang out in the doorway, ready in case Dad has an issue. "Where exactly did you see Parker Watts?" she asks.

I guess she's talking to me again. "Down at the boat."

"I'd prefer you stay away from that boy."

I don't want to get back into it with her, but I can't help myself. "Mom, I'm too old for you to tell me what to do."

"Not as long as you're under my roof."

Before I can point out that the only reason I'm under her roof is because she's asked me to be, the bathroom door opens and Daddy heads toward the bedroom.

Once we get him settled and I give him a kiss good night, I escape to my own room. My shelves are still filled with favorite books, athletic medals, and my prized possession, which is a first-place trophy from the Kent County Waterman's Association Day anchor toss contest the summer after my graduation from high school. After changing into jeans and a clean tank top, I run a brush through my hair and add a touch of lipstick to my lips.

"What are you preening for?" Mom asks when I come down the hall fishing earrings through the holes in my earlobes.

"I'm going up to Waterman's for a beer." I make for the front door.

She follows me outside and whispers so Daddy won't hear her. "Are you meeting Parker Watts?"

"Yes. We've been friends since we were kids."

"That's news to me. Besides, you aren't kids now. It's different."

I begin to walk away.

She grabs my arm. "You need to stay away from him, Kaleigh."

I turn and glare at her. "Why?"

She releases her grip on me. "Never mind why. Just do as I ask."

The evening breeze plays with the wisps of her salt-and-pepper hair. She's only fifty-one, but she looks careworn. I feel sorry for her, but that doesn't stop me from my rebuttal.

"Unless you can give me a good reason, and it has to be the truth, I'll see whomever I want."

"*Whomever*?"

"You always go on the offensive about my education when you have nothing to back up your demands. It's an old trick, Mom. It's not working tonight."

I stalk down the street toward Waterman's with a plan of action in mind and the strong intention of having more than one beer. When I turn the corner, I catch sight of the restaurant roof outlined with lights. The parking lot is full, typical of a summer weekend night.

Once inside, I quickly scan the dining room, although I know that if Parker is still here, he'll be outside on the deck.

Stacey Esposito waves to me. She has waitressed here for years.

"How's your daddy doing?" Stacey asks.

"He's coming along."

"Tell your momma that I'll be happy to sit with him one morning so she can go out and get a mani-pedi or a massage or something to treat herself."

I hug her. "Thanks. I'll let Mom know."

The volume of the music builds as I walk out the doors to the waterfront seating. Junior Wilson and Chatty have the crowd tapping their feet, and I notice Parker leaning over his beer at the dockside bar with one butt cheek on a stool. He's laughing with the bartender. I skirt past crowded tables piled high with steamed crabs. The sound of mallets cracking down on the bay-seasoned crustaceans mixes with the lively conversations of the patrons.

"Hi." I sidle in-between Parker and another customer on the next stool.

"You came." He grins. "What're you drinking?"

I eye his half-empty beer glass. "Same as you."

"Joey, can I have another Natty Boh in a glass?"

The bartender nods.

I glance around and then ask, "Is there someplace quieter? I'd like to talk to you."

Parker frowns.

"It's not bad. It might actually be good for both of us."

Then he raises his eyebrows.

"Not that." I feel myself blush. Although the idea isn't unappealing, I didn't intend to suggest hooking up.

The bartender returns with my cold glass of beer. Parker puts some bills on the bar and steps away with his own glass. "Mind sitting on the edge of the dock?" he asks.

"Perfect."

We navigate around the crowd talking near the bar. On the other side of the tables, the noise level diminishes. We sit with our legs over the edge of the dock, which is crammed with boats owned by folks who traveled by water to find their evening's entertainment and dinner.

Parker's typically cheerful demeanor turns serious. "This is awkward."

I laugh and say, "I'm not proposing that we have sex."

"Oh, good." His eyes widen. "I mean, not that it wouldn't be lit. You're great, Kaleigh."

I kind of enjoy watching him twitch on the line.

He continues, "I'm serious with someone from college."

"That's great, Parker."

"Her name is Ashley. It's not easy being apart for most of the summer, but I don't want to be one of 'those' guys."

"Which guys?" I know exactly what he means, but I was dying to see how he describes them.

"Assholes."

"Oh." I smile to myself. "As I told you, I just ended it with one of them back in LA."

"I say, either be up-front about playing the field or keep your zipper shut."

I snort, nearly shooting beer out of my nose.

Parker looks hurt.

"I'm sorry. I'm not laughing at you or your intentions to be loyal. You just put it in such a funny way. 'Keep your zipper shut.' It's adorable and sincere. You are one of the most sincere guys I've ever known. Your lady is very lucky."

He relaxes. "Thanks. And you deserve to be treated better than what it sounds like this jerk in LA did."

"I appreciate that. I'm sure the right guy is out there." I look out at the harbor, expecting him to walk across the water. It seems like it would take that kind of miracle. "But right now, I have other things on my mind."

"Like?"

"My dad's medical bills are adding up. Someone needs to earn more money, and I know I could do that on the water. My mom is cranky about me taking the *Kaleigh Sue* out by myself; plus, a two-person crew can bring in more crabs." I turn to Parker. "You need a job. What do you think about being my first mate?"

Parker puts his beer down and shakes my hand. "I think it's brilliant."

"Really?"

"As you said, I need a job."

"There's a tiny hitch with the license."

"What's that?"

"I have to convince my father to make me the temporary authorized user. If he does, he's still responsible if I make any violations. I'm not sure he'll be comfortable with that."

While considering this, Parker drinks more of his beer. "If your dad's not going to be able to work anyway, why not ask him to transfer the license over to you? Then it's all on you."

I shake my head. "First, we don't have the spare cash for the fees. And, it might be too much of a blow to his emotional well-being. I don't want him to feel like I'm pushing him out."

Parker nods. "Good thinking. There's no use rubbing his nose in it. You're a very responsible person. He's the one who taught you, so he ought to trust you."

"Here's to hoping." I click my beer glass against Parker's.

Parker insists on walking me home, although he'll have to double back past Waterman's to get to his parents' home on Chesapeake Avenue. We've had a few beers, and it's best that neither of us is driving anywhere.

As we head up South Hawthorne, I ask out of curiosity, "Do you have a car?"

"A small pickup. Need it to get around up at school, but I rarely use it at home."

"In LA, I had to drive everywhere. I hated it."

"So, even if your dad won't give you the okay, and we're back to square one, are you still not going back to Hollywood?"

I laugh. "Why do you keep saying Hollywood instead of LA?"

He glances at me sideways. "Aren't they the same?"

"No, but I appreciate your sarcasm. The answer is I'm staying here. I prefer to walk places."

When we reach my house, he asks, "Can I give you a hug?"

"Sure."

It is brief and a little clumsy.

"Do you think a man and a woman can have a platonic friendship?" he asks.

"Isn't that what you and I have had basically all our lives?"

"I didn't always have pure thoughts about you in high school."

"While I'm flattered, you need to remember that you don't want to be one of 'those' guys."

"Right. My girlfriend, Ashley."

"It'll be best to keep the status quo, especially since we'll be working together."

"Good luck with convincing your dad. Text me."

"I will when I know something."

After shutting the front door, I notice Mom standing in the dining room.

"I told you to stay away from that boy." She stamps into the kitchen.

I know I should just ignore her and go to my room, but I let her irk me. I follow her into the kitchen. "I've asked Parker to crew for me."

"I can't believe you, Kaleigh."

"We've been friends since school. He's a good waterman and an even better person. I can't imagine why you've gone insane about him. It makes absolutely no sense to me."

"Why can't you just trust me on this?" She looks about to explode.

"You're overreacting. I need to know why."

"There's always been bad blood between our families," she blurts out.

I pull my head back. "Bad blood? You've been watching too many reality shows. I know Dad's always had some kind of hang-up about Gus Watts. He was obsessed about beating him at every Watermen's Day competition. He had to haul more oysters and deliver more bushels of crabs, but then, just tonight, he defended the man about his injuries and painkiller addiction. So why are you so upset?"

"I don't want to talk about it." She avoids looking at me.

She's hiding something from me, and the craziest idea comes tumbling out of my mouth. "From the way you're acting, I'd think you were having an affair."

She collapses into one of the kitchen chairs. "I did."

"What?" My voice hits a formerly unknown high pitch. "With whom?"

She slams her hand down on the kitchen table. "With Parker's dad."

There suddenly seems to be less oxygen in the room. "What are you talking about?"

She stands and begins pacing. "When you were less than two years old, I had an affair with Gus Watts."

It takes me a moment to fully entertain the worst possible scenario. "Is Parker my half-brother?"

Her slap stings my cheek. My eyes begin to burn, but I refuse to cry in front of her.

She looks past me. I spin around to see my dad resting on his walker in the doorway. Our arguing has woken him. When I turn to confront her, my mother snatches her car keys and dashes out the back door.

Dad's slippers shuffle across the floor, and he lowers his bulk into a kitchen chair. I'm not sure how much he heard. Did he know about the affair?

I rush to him. "I'm sorry we woke you up."

He struggles to form the sentence. "Your mother is on edge."

"You think?"

He shoots me a look, and his words are slow but perfectly clear. "Keep the sarcasm under control, Kaleigh Sue."

"Yes, sir," I whisper.

"My stroke upset her. She's scared."

"Can I get you anything, Daddy?"

"I'm fine." He pats my arm and deliberately asks, "Do you want to put a cold washrag on your face? It looks sore."

I wipe tears away from my cheeks and sit down. "She's never hit me."

"Like I said, she's not herself. She has a lot to"—he has some difficulty with the 'w' this time—"worry about."

I take my cue. "Which is why I want to crab. I can make money. It'll take some pressure off Mom. It's been a few years since I've worked, but my muscles will get used to it again. Parker is willing to crew with me. Between the two of us, we should do pretty well."

"Your mother's not going to be happy about that."

"My fishing or working with Parker?"

My father doesn't answer.

"Look." I try to reason with him. "She's concerned about me being out there alone, and now I won't be. Dad, I need you to side with me on this."

"You mean, go against your mother?"

"Yes."

His eyes widen.

"I need a license. The cheapest and simplest thing is to make me the temporary authorized user of yours."

He has to slow down to be clear. "But if you do something stupid, it's my responsibility."

"You know I won't violate any regulations. You taught me to do everything by the book."

He puts his hands on the table and pushes himself up. "I'll sleep on it . . . if I can sleep."

"Do you want help?"

He takes hold of his walker and plods toward the bedrooms. "Nope. I'd rather do it myself."

How could she have been unfaithful to a man who believes the sun rises and sets on her? When I think about it, it seemed like he was always trying to make something up to her; shouldn't it have been the other way around?

In the morning, Mom doesn't speak to me when we pass going into and out of the bathroom. I guess I deserve it, but I hope that when she came home last night, Dad told her he's making me the authorized user of his fishing license, and that's why her panties are in a twist.

While I get ready to drive up to Easton for a maid-of-honor gown fitting, of all things, I hear Mom dusting and putting things back down with a thud. She often cleans when she's upset. I guess it makes her feel better, but judging from the amount of noise she's making, I don't think it's helping.

I dig around my room for a smaller purse to carry and take only the essentials from the handbag I brought from California, which could hold a tugboat. On my dresser I spy the lovely antique handkerchief from the bridal shower several days ago. My best friend, Chelsea, is getting married, and her mother bought handkerchiefs at an antique store in Berlin for the shower guests. I put mine into the purse. The bridesmaids are meeting in Easton today for gown fittings and then going out to lunch together.

Chelsea and I met in college, and when we discovered we had grown up just a few miles apart, we clicked. I love Chels, but I'm not in the mood for wedding bells after what my mom revealed last night. Between the parental unit and the pain I suffered after following Dirk the Jerk to LA, I don't think I'll ever be interested in love again.

I dig some good underwear out of my suitcase, which I won't be repacking now. I toss the luggage into the back of my closet. It's a relief not to be flying back west tonight. Originally, I was going to drive a rental car straight to the BWI Airport after the luncheon in Easton. As I apply my makeup, I smile at myself in the mirror. Job free and jerk free. And with a bit of luck, I'll soon be feeling the wind on my face and smelling the bay on the *Kaleigh Sue*.

There's a knock at the door. "Just a minute." I toss on the sleeveless dress I'm wearing today and open the door.

"You look pretty." Dad's speech is clearer this morning.

"Thanks." I kiss his cheek.

He inches his walker past the door and closes it. "I'm making you the," he concentrates on the next word, "authorized user."

"Oh, Daddy!"

"Shhh!"

I scowl at him. "Haven't you told her?"

"Of course I have, but if she hears more about it, I don't think any of the knick-knacks will survive."

"Sometimes if we just do what we want, but we don't parade it in front of her, Mom forgets about it."

He cocks his head. "You know that about her?"

"Sure."

"You're a smart cookie. Yes, so the less said the better. Please, don't talk about Parker. Just catch a lot of crabs."

"We'll do our best."

"Now, we can get you straightened out online at the . . . ," it takes him a moment, "Department of Natural Resources Compass website, but it won't hurt to give Miss Marie a call in Centreville, just to make sure she gets the boat number and your DNR ID number."

"I'm going to be driving through Centreville today to meet Chelsea and the bridesmaids in Easton. I can stop by."

"Good. We want to make sure we have all our ducks in a row before you go out. Now, you also need to go over everything on the boat. She hasn't been run in weeks."

"I checked the engine already."

"Check the oil level. See that the fuel filters haven't accumulated algae after sitting for a while. Check the hose clamps and the engine belts." He looks perkier than I'd seen him since his stroke.

"Dad, I have your checklist. Parker and I will go over everything."

"I hope you don't mind if I report the catches on the FACTS System."

"Of course not. I'm impressed that you're using the new e-reporting system. Aren't you just a man of the twenty-first century?" I put my earrings on.

"I had one of the young 'ellows teach me 'ow to use it." His articulation deteriorates, and he becomes frustrated.

"You're just excited, Dad. So am I. Try slowing down."

He nods and speaks carefully. "The FACTS System is not that difficult." He pauses. "It saves a lot of time, and all my catches and past trips are logged in there, so I can make comparisons or double-check data. I have several things," he thinks for a few seconds, "pre-set, so if you want to change your landing location, you need to let me know. I'll go in and update your crew number since I was working alone."

"This is so exciting, Dad. The three of us will make a great team."

"Your mother?"

I grimace. "No, I meant you, me, and Parker."

"Eventually, we'll w-w-win her over."

I check the time on my phone. "I'd better get going if I want to stop in Centreville on my way."

Daddy takes my hand. "Thanks, honey." He says clearly, "I'm grateful that you're willing to do this."

"Willing? I'm thrilled."

Parker and I go over the *Kaleigh Sue* from top to bottom. We also check all the pots and replace the line to the crab pot buoys where needed. We reference bay maps and charts and ask a million questions of any waterman willing to help a couple of green kids. Dad is pleased to give us all the guidance we want, and we need it. He recommends several places where the crabs had been running weeks ago, but those change with time, tides, temperature, and luck. In the end, we decide to go north for our first trip. We'll work between Worton Point and Howell Point.

On the big morning, my father, as expected, is up at four o'clock in the morning to wish me luck. "You're the fifth gener-ation of Strongs making a living on the water," he reminds me. Mom cooks a huge breakfast for me, just as she always did for Dad. What I don't anticipate is that she's packed a cooler with enough food for me and for Parker. There's two of everything, and I'm touched to think she may be coming around.

It's still dark when I reach the *Kaleigh Sue*. A few minutes later, I hear Parker's pickup pull in. He's brought bait and also picked up two large cups of hot coffee. Because we're both a little nervous, there isn't much conversation. We just get to work preparing to head out.

"All right, let's cut her loose," I say to Parker, who releases the lines.

Once we are out of the harbor, I steer the boat onto the open water where the wooden hull cuts through the chop. First light has broken, but the sun won't breach the horizon for another twenty minutes. I feel my nerves settle as the wind hits my face and the pre-dawn colors splash across the sky. Parker comes over to me, and we both smile from the joy of being out on the bay.

When we reach our destination, I announce, "Show time." I put on my gloves and toss a pair to Parker.

We work in tandem. I bait a pot, Parker tosses it overboard, and from the second steering station on the starboard side, I pull the *Kaleigh Sue* up several feet while he baits the next pot. I pitch it overboard, and Parker pulls the boat up. After setting fifty pots, I drive back to the first crab pot buoy.

"This is it," Parker says as he reaches over the side of the boat with a hook and nabs the line just under the buoy. He puts the line onto the pot puller, which spins the pot up to him. We watch like kids on Christmas morning. There are five crabs inside. We hoot and holler and slap high fives. Parker opens the trap door and shakes the crabs out of the pot and into the hopper. I rebait the trap and toss the pot overboard. Parker pulls the boat up to the next buoy while I measure the crabs and sort them by size. Five-and-a-half-inch males go into a bushel for #1's. The crabs under five inches go into a bushel of #2's. I have to toss one back that's too small. After twenty-five pots are pulled, we switch jobs. We catch some females, or sooks, and Parker starts a bushel for them. Soft shells go into another bushel and peelers into another. By early afternoon, we reach our quota, and Parker heads back down the bay while I text our catch to my dad, who is anxious to hear from me. He texts back that we did well. I feel proud to make him happy.

After offloading the day's catch at the bulkhead area on the east side of Channel Marker 14 in Rock Hall, my shoulders hurt. Each bushel weighs at least forty-five pounds. Eventually, my muscles will get used to this again. When I pull around to our slip, I see my dad sitting on a nearby bench with his walker beside him.

Parker waves to my father. "Guess he couldn't wait until you got home."

While I'm glad to see Dad, I feel unsettled having him watch me back the *Kaleigh Sue* into the slip. Backing up a single-screw boat isn't the easiest thing to do. I nearly ask Parker to take over, but I won't do that. I manage just fine.

Parker lobs the port and starboard bow lines over the corresponding pilings before jumping off. I toss two stern lines to him, and he ties her off.

Dad pulls himself up and pushes his walker across the gravel and down to the boat. "Congratulations!"

I step over the gunwale onto the finger pier and hug him. "Thanks, Dad."

"How'd you do with the buyers?" he asks.

"Fifty percent to restaurants, ten percent public, and forty percent to a dealer."

Parker reaches across to shake my father's hand. "Nice of you to come down to greet us."

"It's an important day, and it was a good one." Dad adjusts his baseball cap while he settles his excitement in order to speak clearly. "I'm happy for you, but remember, they won't always be like this."

"No, sir," Parker answers.

"There's going to be rough weather and no crabs."

I tug on Daddy's arm. "We know that."

"Of course, you do. But tonight's about celebrating. I hope you saved some crabs for us."

Parker offloads two half-full bushels. "All jimmies."

"I hope you don't mind, Dad. I saved some for us and some for Parker's family."

"You might want to bring them all home." Dad has a glint in his eye.

"Dad?" I can't follow where he is headed.

"The families are having a crab feast together tonight at our house."

"Wow." Even Parker seems to find this turn of events surprising.

I am speechless.

Parker starts cleaning up.

"I have to work, Dad."

My father doesn't move. His expression transforms from upbeat to serious.

Parker picks up on this. "I can do it, Kaleigh. Why don't you take your dad home in my truck?"

"We'll walk," Dad says. "But thanks. I do want to talk to Kaleigh."

"Are you sure you want to walk that far?" I slip out of my boots and oilskins.

"Yes. Let's go."

I begin slowly up the pier and across the parking lot with my father.

"Do you have something to explain, Dad? I don't understand how Mom has gone from one end of the sandbar to the other."

He chuckles. "I'm going to tell you the whole story, and then your mom would appreciate it if that's the end of it." He focuses to put the words in the right order. "It's still very painful for her to dredge this up. I'm hoping that once Gus and his wife come over for crabs, it will finally be put to rest."

"Mom called Parker's parents?"

"No. She went to their house."

I'm so surprised that I let out a whistle.

"Now listen, I can only tell you the truth if you agree to accept it and not ask questions of your mother."

What's he going to tell me? "Go on."

"Your mom only told you part of the story because she was protecting me."

"She's the one who ran around. I think you've protected her for years."

His eyes flash his disapproval of either my judgement or interruption—or both. "Why have you spent a year living with that . . . that actor?"

There's no reasonable answer, so I lock my jaw.

"He took you all the way out to California. We didn't even see you this past Christmas because he didn't want to come."

"He had an audition."

"You want to defend that guy at this point?"

"No."

"Instead of thinking with your head, you allowed other parts of your anatomy to make your decisions."

I feel my throat tighten with shame as we go up the street.

"We all make mistakes, including you, daughter. Just remember that."

"Yes, sir."

Daddy's tense expression reveals the amount of concentration it takes to talk this long. "I loved your mother from a distance for years because she and Gus Watts were a serious item. They were in love, but they had issues, like everyone. They decided to take a break. At least, I think that's what they call it now. I took advantage of your mother's vulnerable state, hoping that she'd finally fall in love with me. I wanted her to see that I had more to offer her than Gus Watts." He pauses on the sidewalk and supports himself on his walker. "What happened was she got pregnant with you."

"You had to get married?"

"Yes, and I was thrilled. Your mother put on a good face; however, the real problems started after we were married a year or two. I was drinking too much. I wasn't available," he searches for the word, "emotionally to her. She finally took you and went back to her parents." He sighs and starts pushing his walker again. I can tell this is difficult for him to reveal, so I briefly touch his arm. "While I was trying to put my head on straight, she and Gus had an affair. He was going to leave his wife, but she got pregnant with Parker. Lucky for me, Gus stayed with his family."

"Sounds like Parker's dad was pretty busy, screwing both my mom and his wife."

Dad glowers at me. "The actual timing of this isn't our business. Maybe Mrs. Watts was pregnant before her husband had the affair with your mom. It was very brief, and their plans to divorce us and marry one another didn't last long before Mrs. Watts found out she was expecting. But he was still with his wife, so maybe he was having sex with her, too." He has to think. "Nevertheless, he reneged on his promise to your mother. It took several more months for me to convince your mom to come home. I got sober and have stayed so right up until now."

My father's drive to outdo Gus Watts commercially and then his sudden change of heart toward the man now made sense. "You understand Mr. Watts' opioid addiction."

"I do sympathize with what he's going through." Dad shakes his head. "And to have to sell his boat. We'd all cut off our right arms first."

"I know."

"Now, Kaleigh. Go easy on your mom. If I'm lucky and don't have another stroke, she's facing thirty or more years of taking care of me. I'll get better, but I won't be the same. This isn't exactly how we pictured our golden years."

"Does she love you, Daddy?"

"She's stuck by me. She's sticking by me now when I have even less to offer her."

Since Daddy avoids answering my question, I'll just have to ask Mom.

As the grown-ups continued with their mallet smacking out on our screened back porch, Parker and I take our beers around to the front stoop. Our parents' laughter can still be heard all the way around the house.

I take a swig of my beer before settling my butt on the warm cement step. "Who would have guessed?"

"Really." Parker sits next to me. His long legs stretch out in front of him. "I'm happy about it."

"Me, too. I just can't get over how well they're all getting along after these years of 'bad blood' as my mom called it. Do you know the truth?" I ask Parker.

"I don't need to know."

I look at him. "You're such a 'guy.'"

He scratches his nose. "I hope so."

"Listen, I have a wedding coming up, and I'm the maid-of-honor. Would you consider asking Ashley if she would be comfortable with you going with me as a friend? I mean, if you don't mind. I hate facing the whole ordeal without a 'date.'" I make air quotations to be completely clear.

"I don't mind, and I think Ashley would be cool with it, but I have a better idea."

"Go on."

"I have a friend, a shipwright from St. Michaels. He's a little older."

"I've sworn off men, but I could reconsider for someone more mature, that's for sure."

"He's a good guy. I guess he's attractive because I've seen girls get all goo goo over him, but he carried a torch for his high school sweetheart for years."

"That doesn't sound very encouraging."

"Keep your oilskins on. The girl had to go discover the world, but they agreed to meet in ten years at an old abandoned place they'd fantasized about owning and fixing up when they were teenagers. When he showed up there earlier this summer, she had bought and rehabbed the cottage for him. She's some hotshot with tons of money. She won't give up her career for him, but she wanted to thank him for being her first love."

"You're going to make me weep."

"I know. Anyway, they said their goodbyes for good, and he's finally ready to move on. I think you'd like him."

"Parker Watts, you're matchmaking."

He laughs. "I guess I am. You and Evan are great people. I'd like you both to be happy like Ashley and me. Who knows, maybe you'll click."

I gently slap his forearm. "You are too sweet."

"So, should I tell Evan about you?"

"Hell, yeah."

After Dad is asleep, Mom and I finish cleaning up from the crab feast.

"You should get to bed, Kaleigh. I can do this. You have to get up early for your second day as a waterwoman." Her eyes are glistening, and the corners of her mouth are inching up as she shuts the refrigerator.

"You're proud of me, aren't you?"

"Always." She takes my hands. "I'm so sorry I slapped you."

The dam I've been holding in for so long suddenly breaks.

"Oh, Kaleigh." Mom wipes my wet cheeks. "Please forgive me. I've never done that before, and I still can't believe I did."

I shake my head. "It's not that. I'm sorry I didn't come home after college. Maybe Daddy wouldn't have had the stroke if I had been here helping like I planned."

"Don't blame yourself. This isn't your fault."

"It's why I wanted to start fishing so badly. I want to make this up to you and to Daddy."

"I won't let you take on that responsibility." She hands me some tissues from a box on the counter. "Tell me you won't keep beating yourself up for something none of us had any control over."

I mumble, "Okay," while I blow my nose.

"We need to look at the blessings that are coming from this difficulty. You're home and working on *Kaleigh Sue*. Your father and I are closer. I'm finally putting down something that has haunted me for years." She grabs a tea towel and starts drying dishes from the rack.

Dad told me not to ask her anything, but I have to. "I need to ask one question."

She sighs and puts down the plate she was about to put in the cabinet. "Go ahead."

"Do you love Dad? Have you ever loved him? Do you love Mr. Watts?"

"That's three questions."

I stand firm.

She puts her hand on one hip. "Hasn't your father always said that actions speak louder than words?"

"Yes."

"If I didn't love your father, why would I watch for him every day when he was fishing? God, I couldn't wait to see him walking up the street toward home. Why would I be taking care of him now?"

"True."

"I don't think about Gus Watts as anything more than an old friend. Your dad is the love of my life. He is and so are you." She pulls me into her arms.

"Thanks, Mom."

"I just thought being friends with the Watts' would be awkward. I was overreacting."

"Like usual." I smile at her.

"Wiseass." She swipes at my nose and picks up the plate and puts it away. "Anyway, when I went over there to set things straight, they didn't want to talk about it, either. 'Water over the dam,' Parker's mom said. And they thought celebrating our children's business partnership with a crab feast from their first catch was a great idea."

"I'm so relieved."

"Me, too." She sits down and dabs her forehead. "I must be flashing."

"You've had a lot of stress. Oh, Stacey Esposito offered to stay with Dad so you can go get a massage or a manicure."

"That's sweet. I'd like to take her up on that, but your father won't want a babysitter."

I put away the last dishes. "I'm bushed."

"Kaleigh, sometime soon I want to take you out to a fancy lunch. Maybe over to the Inn at Osprey Point. They have a lovely restaurant."

"That would be nice, Mom. What about Daddy?"

"He thinks he'll be up to it soon."

"Or maybe Stacey could check on him, and we could have a girls' afternoon out."

Mom stands up and hugs me again. This is the most hugging I've gotten from her in years, and I could get used to it.

Homeward Migration

M Y FATHER DANGLED A stained pillowcase containing my kitten over Assateague Channel. He'd tossed in a brick to make sure it would sink to the bottom.

We stood in the pre-dawn darkness at the edge of the causeway between Chincoteague and Assateague Islands.

"Tell me you'll never do it again." He removed three fingers so that only his thumb and index finger held on to the one and only thing I loved in this world.

Tears streamed down my face. I clawed at his muscular arm holding the dingy sack over the point where the water was the deepest. My kitten had stopped mewing. She might already be dead.

"Say it!" he snarled.

"I promise." I continued helplessly to grasp for the fabric. "Daddy, please don't drown Angel." I sucked the snot running from my nose back down my throat and choked on it.

"I can't hear you."

"Don't kill her." I didn't even know what I'd done this time to set him off. "I promise I'll never do it again."

"Damn right you won't." He let go of the pillowcase. The dull white fabric billowed and disappeared under the water. "Now, get in the truck."

First light broke over Assateague. The sun wouldn't shine through the cloud cover this morning, but in about twenty minutes, it would still rise over the beach as it had every day of my ten years on this planet. The dawn was one thing I could count on.

"I had the drowning dream again, Dr. Lessing." I look around her stylish Philadelphia office. The built-in oak bookcases are filled with volumes on psychology, mental health, and therapy. There are no figurines or photographs. It's strictly business with Dr. Lessing.

Dr. Lessing crosses her legs. "Anything different?"

"I don't think so. I am in the pillowcase and the water is rushing in. I claw at the fabric but can't get out."

"And you were nine years old when your father did this to your kitten?"

"Ten." She knows how old I was. I've told her my age a few dozen times over the year and a half that I've been in therapy with her. Sometimes I feel like she asks the same questions to see if I'll change my answers.

"Have you given any more consideration to going back to Chincoteague Island?"

"What good would that do?" I resist picking at a rough nail cuticle.

"You tell me."

I sigh. Why won't she answer my question? Why does she always turn it back on me? "No good at all. I haven't gone back in twenty years, and I don't see the point of going now."

She writes something down on her notepad, which annoys me. Why am I still coming to her for therapy? I think that's the bigger question.

"What are you thinking?" she asks.

"I'm wondering why I'm still in therapy with you."

"Why are you?"

I rise and cross the distance between us to shake her hand. "I'm not any longer."

She takes my hand. "Good luck, Becca."

"You, too, Dr. Lessing. Goodbye."

I grin all the way to the elevator and down to my car parked in a garage off Rittenhouse Square. There are still remnants of that smile as I maneuver along the Schuylkill Expressway, and no one smiles on that highway. I hum to myself all the way along City Avenue, past Saint Joseph's University, and pull into my driveway on Overbrook Avenue.

When I reach into my mailbox, there's an envelope from a lawyer in Chincoteague, Virginia, and my hands shake as I open it right on the porch. My father has died. Wouldn't that just send Dr. Lessing into therapeutic ecstasy? But since I haven't had any contact with my father since I was sixteen years old, I feel only relief that he's gone. The lawyer explains that he is handling the interment, thank God. I'm not going to pretend at a funeral that the man was anything but a sick bastard. My knees weaken when I read further. I sit on a rocker. The lawyer states that I need to come to his office on Chincoteague Island to sign some papers. There's the house—the shack, really. There's the will. There's a letter. *Fuck.*

My appointment with the lawyer is at one o'clock. When I called, he insisted on the phone that this couldn't be done through the mail. My plan is to drive down in the morning, sign whatever, and drive home. I set my alarm for seven o'clock. If I'm on the road by eight, I'll get to Chincoteague by noon. On the eleven o'clock news there's mention of a hurricane coming up the coast, and for a moment, I think I have an excuse to cancel.

However, the forecast suggests that it's going to go out to sea, so I turn off the TV and crawl into bed.

I toss and turn after dreaming that I'm drowning in a pillowcase. I'd hoped the dream would stop or change now that he's dead, but no such luck. There's no way I'm getting back to sleep, so I take a shower. Since I'm wide awake, I jump into my car and head south. When I'm crossing from Maryland into Virginia, I realize I'll be in Chincoteague before the sun rises. Should I listen to Dr. Lessing and dare risk facing my nightmare? Several times she brought up the possibility that I go back to Chincoteague, to Oyster Bay specifically, and confront my father. "When ponies walk on water," I had told her.

When Chincoteague Road curves past the high fencing around the NASA facility on the left and the Wallops Island National Wildlife Refuge on the right, I take a swig of water from the metal bottle I filled before leaving. There's just enough light in the sky to feel the day is beginning when I drive the first causeway over marshes and Mosquito Creek. I cross open water when I hit Queen Sound Channel. Chincoteague Bay lies in the dark to the north. On the next stretch of causeway, my headlights bounce off a series of large, wooden road signs advertising everything from restaurants to construction companies. How can they mar the natural beauty along this stretch with commercialism? The causeway makes a dramatic curve over Black Narrows, and The Tump comes into view in the East. Tumps are the clumps or mounds of grasses and shrubs rising out of the wetland. Chincoteague has lots of these clumps, so native Chincoteaguers, or Teaguers, affectionately refer to their island as The Tump.

I grip the steering wheel as I drive over the drawbridge into town. If I turn left on Main Street toward Oyster Bay, I'll be heading to the childhood house I escaped at sixteen. Instead, I go straight.

All along Maddox Boulevard, I'm amazed by how much commerce has sprung up in twenty years. There are stores and restaurants and take-out stands and motels everywhere. After going through the light at Chicken City Road and around the traffic circle where the Chamber of Commerce building now sits, I continue on Maddox until I reach the Assateague Channel. Anxiety churns up in my stomach when I see the brown sign with white lettering for Chincoteague National Wildlife Refuge and Assateague Island National Seashore. I force down the bile rising in my throat when I approach the spot where I realized how mentally ill my father was. It took me another six years to escape, but I had. I never intended to return.

The refuge gates are open. The sign states the park is open from five o'clock in the morning until ten at night. As I drive along Beach Access Road, I see a few other vehicles carrying early risers who perhaps plan to scour the beach for shells, photograph the sunrise, or fish. I find it comforting that I'm not alone out here with my memories.

The paved road cuts through a wooded area past the signs for the lighthouse and the educational center. The view breaks open over marsh and ponds. It's too early for any of the ponies from the south herd to be out eating, but I expect to spot some later in the morning. The scenery intermittently shifts from woods to bog along the way to the beach until the view opens up to the Atlantic Ocean. I pull around a sand-covered traffic rotary and go into the parking lot to the north, which holds only three other vehicles. The sun hasn't broken the horizon, but it is painting the sky and sea with streaks of pink and orange. I step out of my car, take off my sandals, and sigh as I sink my feet into the cool sand. It suddenly strikes me that I haven't seen the ocean in twenty years. My vacations have all been to the mountains or lakes. I suck the salty air into my lungs. It's the best smell in the world.

A white-haired gentleman with a camera on a tripod seems to be waiting for the next shift in the sky as the sun gets closer to appearing. Meanwhile, he's scanning the edge of the water with a pair of binoculars. There's a flock of shorebirds racing back and forth with the surf as they feed on small organisms in the sand. I remember that my mother told me they were sanderlings. A wave disturbs most of them, and they call a short *kwit, kwit, kwit* as they fly in close formation, circle over the surf, and land a few yards away. The little birds bring back comforting memories of my mother. She frequently brought me out here to learn about the birds. I was eight the last time I'd observed sanderlings. Mom died the following winter.

I hear the man laugh and notice he has his binoculars pointed at two sanderlings that are duking it out. One of the little birds flies into the other and knocks it over just as a small wave nearly engulfs them. The downed bird pokes its beak at the aggressor as it hops back onto its black feet. Both birds tumble over one another in the wet sand. I wander closer because I don't remember seeing the small shorebirds behave this way. The man looks at me.

"Why are they fighting?" I ask.

"Hormones. Like teenage boys." He has kind eyes.

"But it's not spring. Aren't they going to migrate soon?"

He nods. "Yes. Maybe it's the drop in their breeding hormones that sets them off. Some of them are still protecting their territory."

"It's sort of comical."

"Have you been here before?" he asks and looks back through the viewfinder of his camera. The sun is peeking over the ocean. The colors in the water and clouds intensify and broaden, and he presses the shutter a few times.

"Yes, but it was a long time ago."

I'm not sure if he's a local or a tourist. He's wearing a photographer's vest and has his baseball cap on backward. If he's a Teaguer, he may know or know of my father. I don't want to get into that story.

"Jim?" A woman calls from the section of Swans Cove Pond that runs behind the beach. She's waving for him to come over with one hand while still holding her binoculars up to her eyes with her other hand.

"Come meet my wife." He sprints over, and I follow.

"It's a roseate spoonbill!" Her voice is exuberant as she points to a tall bird with long legs standing in the shallow water.

"You've got to be kidding," her husband says.

"It must have been blown up here by the storm." She hands me her binoculars like it's the most natural thing to do.

"Thank you." I focus on the bird with its pink wings and long, spoon-shaped beak, which is sweeps from side to side in the water to catch food. "Is it young? Is that why it got off course?"

The man takes another look before dashing back to his camera. "I think it's a second-year bird. Brighter pink than an immature, but not adult plumage yet."

"We're likely to see a lot of unusual birds because of the storm that's coming," the woman says.

I lower her binoculars and really look at her face for the first time. She's beautiful with laugh lines and crystal-blue eyes. I guess she's in her mid to late sixties.

"I'm Becca."

She takes my hand. "I'm Lisa, and that's Jim. Can I have another look?"

I pass her glasses back. "Sure."

She examines the roseate spoonbill again. "This is so exciting!" She slings the strap of her binoculars over her shoulder and pulls out her cell phone. "If I can get any reception out here, I'll post this on the rare bird list. This baby is going to be a celebrity for as long as it stays." She begins texting a message into her phone. "In the old days, we had to decide if we were willing to rush home and make a phone call on the landline. It was hard to leave the bird. It could be gone by the time we got back or when other birders reached the location. That's how Jim began photographing. He wanted proof of what we saw in case anyone questioned our call."

When the colors on the pond shift, I turn around. The rising sun is shooting shafts of gold into the ocean from behind dark clouds. "Oh, look at that."

"What a morning." Lisa puts her cell away. "I don't know whether to watch the eastern sky or the roseate spoonbill."

Jim jogs back to take photographs of the spoonbill. The wind whips up, and he nearly loses his baseball cap. "The chop is increasing from the hurricane."

"Hurricane? I heard it was going out to sea."

"Not now. That's why the surf is becoming so wild." Jim adjusts his camera's focus when the bird moves a few feet closer. He fires off several shots. "They thought it was going out to sea and would just skirt us, but in the middle of the night, the storm changed course."

"It's going to be a rough one." Lisa lifts her binoculars to her eyes. "Where do you live?"

"Oh, I don't live here. Well, not anymore."

"Do you have a hotel room?" Lisa lowers her glasses.

"No. I'm leaving this afternoon."

"How far do you have to drive to get home?"

"Lisa?" Jim keeps his eye on his viewfinder.

"My husband thinks I ask too many questions, but I think people can always tell me to mind my own business if they don't want to answer." The wind swirls some of her silver hair around her face. She tucks it back behind her ears.

"I live in the Overbrook area of Philadelphia."

Lisa questions, "You drove down here in the middle of the night?"

"Sort of. My father died, and I'm meeting with the lawyer. Then I'm driving back to Philly this afternoon."

Lisa's expression transitions to one of sympathy. "I'm sorry for your loss."

"Thanks." I feel like telling her it's no loss, but I don't want to be rude.

"Who's your dad?" Jim asks.

"Jim?" Lisa teases her husband, and he looks at her with nothing short of glowing eyes.

Clearly, they are still in love, and my heart aches to know that kind of sureness. "My father was Zachary Culver."

Jim and Lisa exchange a quick and telling glance. They knew him.

"I forgot he had a daughter," Lisa says.

"I left when I was sixteen."

"Our youngest son might be about your age. Did you know Ben Cooper?"

I've tried to forget so much that I lost even the good things. "Ben Cooper doesn't ring a bell, but he could have been in my class at school."

"He and his children recently moved back to the Eastern Shore from Manhattan."

"Well, I'm getting hungry. Want to join us for breakfast?" Jim begins putting his camera into a bag and closing up his tripod.

"Have you ever had Sandy Pony Donuts?" Lisa licks her lips.

"No."

"Do you like donuts, or do you want a full breakfast?" Jim asks.

"Donuts sound fine."

"You can follow us, but just in case, the donut truck is on the left before the traffic circle."

As we walk to our cars, Lisa says, "They have twenty-four different flavors."

"That's a lot of choices."

Jim loads his camera equipment in the back seat of their Jeep. "Great coffee, too."

I follow them out of the national park, along Maddox Boulevard, and into a parking lot with a light-blue food truck. A white horse holding a donut in one hoof is painted on the side. There is already a line of people waiting. I peruse the twenty-four flavors, most of which are surprising. Jim orders a donut called the Porky Pony that comes with bacon on top. Lisa goes for the Charlie Brown, which has a peanut butter glaze and mini chocolate chips. I decide to try the Sea Foam topped with coconut.

"This is scrumptious." I lean against my car with a cup of coffee balancing on the hood.

"I know." Lisa smiles and takes another bite of her donut.

Jim blows on his coffee in one hand and nibbles on the donut in the other hand.

An alert signal chimes on Lisa's phone. She sets everything down, reaches into their car, and checks her cell. "This hurricane is going to really ramp up this afternoon and tonight. They may close the causeway across Chesapeake Bay."

I cringe. "That means I might not be able to get out of here after the meeting with my father's lawyer."

"Come stay with us." Lisa gently tosses her cell onto the car seat. "You're welcome to use our guest room, or if you want more privacy, there's the bunkhouse. Our sons used it as teenagers. Our grandchildren use it now whenever they visit."

"Aren't you going to evacuate?" I wrap the rest of my donut in the napkin.

"If they tell us to go, we will, but it's not supposed to be that bad." Jim has obviously lived through many hurricanes and nor'easters out here. "Some flooding and high winds. We put the house and the bunkhouse up on pilings after Sandy. We did evacuate for that super storm, and the damage was extensive."

My cell phone chimes. I glance at the text.

"I don't believe it."

"Something wrong?" Lisa asks. The sincerity in her eyes deflates my anger a bit.

"The lawyer is postponing our appointment until tomorrow or the day after that. He's a volunteer fireman, and it's all hands on deck with this hurricane coming."

Lisa loops her arm inside my arm. I don't usually like people getting into my space, but it actually feels reassuring. "You must stay with us. We have plenty of food."

"I didn't bring any clothes other than the ones I'm wearing. Maybe I should just drive back to Philly and come back after the storm passes."

Jim takes off his baseball cap and scratches his head. "You do whatever you think is best, but you'd be driving close to the coast until Wilmington. The storm could make that pretty hairy."

I sigh.

Lisa pats my arm before releasing it. "Come on. Stay with us. We can loan you some clothes for the night."

"Do you live near Oyster Bay?" I ask with a tremor in my voice.

"Out near your father's place? No. We're close to Memorial Park."

Before I get my car door open, Lisa says, "You'll be surprised by all the new homes built out near your dad's. It's a real neighborhood now."

I pull my car door shut. I have no intention of going out there. They lead the way in their Jeep, and I am relieved to turn south off Maddox Boulevard.

After dinner, Jim and Lisa lose power. The wind howls around, above, and below their cottage. There are moments when I think we may be lifted off the pilings and end up in Oz.

"If you don't mind, I will stay in your guest room instead of out in the bunkhouse."

Lisa smiles. "Good. I don't want to be worrying about you out there all night by yourself."

Headlights flash across the ceiling. Jim goes to the window. "Someone's coming."

"Who is it?" Lisa pulls on a sweater.

"The wind is driving the rain too hard to tell. It must be someone official. There a red light pulsing on top of the pickup."

"I hope they're okay." Lisa lights another candle.

Jim opens the door when the officials are right outside. The wind nearly rips the door out of his hands. "Hurry in."

The men, both wearing Chincoteague Volunteer Fire Company coats, are about twenty years apart in age. The older of the two stamps his feet on the mat inside the front door. "Sorry to bring water into your place, Jim."

Jim shakes the man's hand. "Andy, I couldn't make out who the two of you were in the storm. It must have been hell getting out here."

The younger guy stares at me. I guess he's around my age and looks familiar, but I can't place him.

"Rosie?" he says.

His voice and the name take me back. The only person to use my middle name, which was my mother's name, was Billy. After Mom died, he started calling me Rosie.

"Billy?"

He grins, revealing smile lines around his brown eyes.

No one else speaks in the candlelit room. I can feel the older folks staring at us. They must be wondering what will happen next. I'm not sure what to do, but Billy crosses the room, sopping water across the floor. He wraps his strong arms around me. My mind tells me to pull away, but my body clings to him.

"I'm sorry I'm all wet," he whispers.

"I don't care."

Billy had a license and his older brother's truck, so he drove me off the island to a bus station when I escaped Oyster Bay. He promised to keep an eye on my dad. I told him not to bother. Although that was a lifetime ago, I don't want to end this drippy hug.

He looks into my eyes before releasing me. "Becca Rose Culver, this is Anderson Vaughn." He gestures to the older fireman.

"Andy." He shakes my hand. "I'm your father's lawyer."

"The only person willing to deal with old Culver." Billy's eyes flash.

"Bill and I are both volunteer firemen." Andy chuckles. "Well, I suppose you guessed that." He gestures to their gear. "When I told Bill that you were on the island to settle your father's estate, he insisted we come out here immediately. I'm glad you texted me about where you were staying, or we'd be scouring all of Chincoteague right now."

"I have some lukewarm coffee if you boys would like to warm up a little." Lisa picks up the flashlight to find her way into the kitchen.

"Thank you, but we can't stay." Andy steps back to the door. "We need to continue checking each road, stopping at houses to make sure people are okay."

Billy takes my hand. "Maybe I could see you tomorrow?"

"I'm leaving tomorrow." I turn to Andy, hoping he'll confirm our meeting and not put it off another day.

"Until we have power, I can't have you in my office, Becca." Andy stamps more wet off his boots onto the mat, but I wonder if he's eager to get Billy moving.

Billy, who is still holding my hand, says, "I'll take you out to your dad's place tomorrow."

"No! I'm not going out there."

Billy hesitates. I watch him pick his words. "We'll talk in the morning." He looks at Jim and Lisa. "You folks okay? Do you need anything?"

Jim walks him to the door. "We're fine, Bill. Thanks for checking."

Andy and Billy dash back into the wind. Two candles are extinguished by the wind coming in. Jim has to lean into the door to shut it. He turns the bolt. The headlights revolve across the ceiling and wall as the truck turns and goes back out the road.

About half an hour later, the wind lets up a little. Jim grabs a large flashlight and his rain jacket. "I'm going to survey how things are holding up outside."

"I'd rather you sit tight with us." Lisa kisses his cheek.

Jim opens the door. "I'll be careful."

"How long have you and Jim been married?" I sit on the sofa.

"Forty-six years." Lisa sits at a nearby window. She tracks the beam of her husband's flashlight. "Billy seems happy to see you."

"We went all through school together until I left."

"Our son is older than you and Billy. That's why I didn't remember you and even forgot that Zachary Culver had a daughter." She looks regretful. "I would have tried to help you. Especially after your mother died."

I don't know what to say to her.

Lisa directs her full attention on me. "Zach Culver wasn't right in the head."

"You have no idea."

"Well, I do a little. I didn't grow up here. Jim did. When we were first married, I moved here to a little place Jim and I bought up the road from your daddy's. Zach's parents were dead, and his siblings had all moved off island. He was all alone out there and really still a kid. Even though the houses were far apart, we couldn't stay there long. He was a very difficult neighbor. After I got pregnant, we stayed over with Jim's parents for a while. No one wanted to purchase our house. But eventually a developer bought it. For years, he couldn't do anything with it, though."

"Because of my father."

Lisa nods.

"How he lured my mother out there is baffling." A chill runs down my spine. "I don't want to talk about him anymore, Lisa."

"I understand." She stands up. "Here comes Jim."

I wake up when my phone chimes. It's a text from Andy asking if he can give my cell number to Billy. I answer *Sure*. I appreciate the lawyer's professionalism.

The power is still out, but daylight is arriving. I peek out the window next to the bed in Lisa and Jim's guestroom. The hurricane has moved on, and I can see downed branches and limbs everywhere.

By the time I'm dressed in yesterday's clothes, my phone chimes again. Billy has been up all night. He's showered and wants to come pick me up.

"Not to go to Oyster Bay," I text back.

"10-4."

I laugh. As kids, we were both hooked on the *Smokey and the Bandit* movies with Burt Reynolds and Sally Fields. We started saying "10-4" to each other on a regular basis.

"How did you sleep?" Lisa asks when I wander into her kitchen.

"Okay but not great. When the wind picked up again, it was so loud."

"I know." Her phone chimes. "It's my son Ben. He's worried." She texts something to him.

"Billy texted me. He's coming over."

"Good." She puts her phone down. "Hopefully it won't be long before we get our power back. Meanwhile, I think the orange juice stayed chilled. I didn't open the refrigerator once we lost power. Would you like some?"

"I would. Thank you." I sit at her table.

She opens and shuts the refrigerator door in a flash, trying to preserve her food. "Jim's outside cleaning up."

"Anything bad?"

"No. A lot of limbs are down. Some flooding, but we're very lucky." She hands me a large glass of orange juice. "Drink it up before it gets warm."

I take a few sips. It's refreshing. "So Billy is a saltwater cowboy."

"He joined the fire company as soon as he was old enough."

"Is Billy married?"

Lisa sits with me. "He was. It didn't work out. He met her at college. She couldn't hack it out here."

"I'm sorry."

"It's not for everyone."

"Absolutely not. It's not easy. How did you and Jim make a living?" I begin to gobble down the juice.

"Jim worked for NASA as an electrical engineer over on Wallops Island."

"Was it hard for you to adjust to living out here?"

"At first. Once I had the boys, they kept me busy. I had a nursing degree, so after the youngest was in school, I worked with a local doctor in town until I retired. Now I volunteer at the library."

I'm surprised when I realize I've polished off the juice.

"Want some more?" Lisa asks.

"I guess I'm hungry."

Lisa goes to the counter. "I wish we'd thought to buy more Sandy Pony donuts yesterday. All I have are store bought." She brings over a plate of sugar donuts and pours me more juice.

"Thanks for taking me in."

"It's nice to have you here. In fact, Jim and I talked last night about you staying in the bunkhouse for as long as you'd like. Ben and his children won't be coming back out here until the holidays. Once school starts, they're so busy."

"Oh." I find her generosity overwhelming. "I need to get home, but thank you."

"Have to go back to work, I guess." She sits and nibbles at a donut.

"Well, actually I work from home."

I can tell that my admission fuels Lisa's plan to have me stay. "There's a bathroom out there and a little kitchenette. We used to use it as a vacation rental."

The light hanging over the table comes on. "Hallelujah!" Lisa claps her hands. The refrigerator begins to hum.

Jim and Billy walk in the door together.

"Look who's returned. He cleans up pretty well," Jim jokes.

Billy is handsome all showered and shaved, but there was nothing wrong with how he looked in his fireman's coat and his dark, wet hair plastered to his head.

"The power is back." Lisa continues to clap.

"Thank God." Jim plugs the coffeemaker in and starts to make a pot of java.

Before I can say anything to Billy, my phone chimes. "Andy is going into his office and wants me to come in."

"I'll drive you over, and then we can find some lunch, since things will be opening up soon."

After two detours around downed trees and flooded streets, we reach Andy's office.

As soon as we go in, I ask, "Do you mind if Billy sits in on our meeting?"

Andy slaps Billy on the back. "Do you trust him?" He winks at me.

"Completely."

"Have a seat." Andy relaxes in his chair behind his large, wooden desk, which has several piles of folders spread over it.

Billy and I sit across from Andy, who hands me some papers. "Your father has left everything to you, and this is an offer to buy your dad's place."

"This offer looks generous to me," I tell him.

"The developer who's built all those new homes out by your father's property has been chomping at the bit to get ahold of it. Frankly, it's an eyesore, and I'm sure he'll just bulldoze it. How do you feel about that, Becca?" Andy asks.

"Torch it. Blow it up. I don't care." I uncross and cross my legs in the opposite direction.

Andy writes down some notes. "Okay. So, you'll accept his offer?"

"Yes."

"Now, is there anything you want out of the house? I'd be happy to take you out there myself."

"If you want to go, Rosie, I'll take you," Billy says.

"No. There's nothing there that I want."

"Okay. There's one last thing." Andy pulls an envelope out of a folder and slides it across his desk to me.

Rebecca Rose Culver is printed on the front of it in my father's handwriting.

"I don't want that."

Andy's eyes fill with empathy. "He said you'd feel that way, but he insisted I give it to you."

Out of respect for Andy, I pick it up and shove it into my handbag. I won't read it, but Andy can feel that he did his duty.

"Is that it?" I ask.

"Yes."

I stand, and both men rise to their feet. I reach across the desk and shake Andy's hand. "Thank you for handling everything. I hope I wasn't too difficult."

The lawyer walks Billy and me to the door. "Not at all. I'll be in touch when the property sale is settled and I have the payment for you."

"I appreciate it."

On the street, Billy takes my hand as if no time has passed. I'm surprised by how good it feels.

Billy gives my hand a squeeze before opening his truck door for me. "Will you let me take you to lunch before you leave?"

I check my phone. I have time before I'll hit the rush-hour traffic on Route 95. "Sure. That would be nice."

"Do you like tacos?"

"Love them."

"I know just the place. Pico Taqueria." He bounds around to the driver's side, and we head back onto Maddox.

There's a huge tree branch blocking the road, but Billy takes another route. After several extra minutes, we pull up to a take-out restaurant that consists of a few trailers connected together with temporary roofing over the side where you place your order. We step around large puddles to reach the side window where we pick up our food.

"I have a place in mind to eat." Billy starts his truck.

"This smells so good, I'm not sure I can wait."

As we cruise along Main Street, shopkeepers are beginning to open up. There's a gentleman clearing debris away from the front of what appears to be a bookstore.

Billy pulls over, "Need help, Jon?"

"No thanks, Billy."

"Jon, this is Rosie."

"Hello. Quite a mess, isn't it?" He holds up some soggy leaves.

"How long have you had your bookstore?" I ask.

"My wife and I opened Sundial Books in 2007."

"Any damage inside?" Billy asks.

The bookstore owner gestures into the building fronted with large glass windows. "Not sure. Jane's inside checking for water, but I think we're fine."

"Text me if you need anything." Billy shifts into drive.

"Nice to meet you," I say.

Jon waves as we pull away.

"There's an independent bookstore in Chincoteague?" I silently hope there's time to explore it before I need to leave.

A little smile twitches on Billy's lips. "Miracles never cease."

"Well, it wasn't here when I left."

"Things have changed, Rosie."

Billy slows but continues driving through a section of flooded road on our way out to Curtis Merritt Harbor.

"Do you think we'll have to get out and swim?" I giggle.

"This truck can get through most anything."

It does, and he parks in front of a row of fishing boats. He points to a boat with the name "Rosie" painted on the hull.

"That's mine." He grins.

"Oh, Billy." I'm so touched that I can't say another word.

"I'll take you aboard after we eat."

"I'd like that."

We eat in the truck, and balancing my meal in my lap isn't easy since it consists of the biggest, most unusual tacos ever.

"I'm glad you grabbed extra napkins." I wipe my mouth after taking a bite out of a Chincoteague Classic Taco with fish, lettuce, pico de gallo, cotija cheese, and crème fraiche.

Billy sinks his teeth into his second taco, which is called The Maddox, a cornmeal-fried local oyster with pickled carrots, daikon, tartar sauce, and Thai basil.

When I laugh, he admits, "I still eat too fast."

"A product of being the youngest of seven. You were always afraid someone older would grab your portion. How is your family?"

"Everyone is good. Mom and Dad are still in the old house. Mary Grace is a science teacher here at the high school. Pat and I have the boat. We fish for a living. The twins moved off island. They live near each other in New Hampshire. They bring their families out for a vacation each year. John and his family live in DC. Kathy is in Salisbury, Maryland. She works at the zoo." Billy takes another bite of his lunch. "Mmm."

"I know. I've never tasted tacos like this before."

Billy wipes his hands with a napkin and asks, "Do you remember my little cousin Chelsea?"

"Was she the toddler who came to visit with her parents and older sisters for a few weeks every summer?"

"Yeah. My mom's sister. Aunt Ellen and Uncle Ron."

"Chelsea was adorable!"

"She's getting married in a couple of weeks."

"No way! How can she be old enough?"

"She graduated college with a degree in finance. She's become my advisor."

"That's great." I decide to pick up on the wedding thread of our conversation. "Lisa told me you were married, but things didn't work out."

"No, it didn't." Billy takes a swig of his soda.

"Have you been serious with anyone else?"

"On and off, but nothing long-term." He puts the soda bottle in the holder and looks at me. "What about you?"

"It's never been worth the risk."

"I'm sorry."

"Don't be. I'm fine."

He glances at my handbag. "What are you going to do with the envelope?"

"I'll probably burn it."

"You honestly aren't curious?"

"Not one bit."

"Do you mind if I read it?"

Billy had been through everything with me. My father was beastly to him, too. Billy's mother fed me when I had nothing to eat. I even bunked with Mary Grace and Kathy when I had to stay out of the house. I figure Billy has a right to see it. "Go ahead, if you want."

He pinches the edge of the envelope that is sticking out of my bag. He takes a deep breath before tearing it open. There's a single piece of folded paper. Billy unfolds it and reads what my father wrote. "Wow."

"Oh, for God's sake!"

"Sorry." Billy apologizes because he knows he's been caught.

"You did that on purpose to make me want to read it."

"It's only one sentence. It won't take you long."

"Go ahead. Read it."

Billy doesn't even look back at the paper. "Forgive me, daughter."

"Bullshit. It doesn't say that."

I snatch it from him.

Forgive me, daughter.

My hands shake. The letter floats to the floor. Billy removes the remains of our lunches from his lap and mine so he can hold me in his arms. I sob into his solid chest for a long time. He says nothing, but I feel his hand gently patting my back.

When I can speak I say, "I don't think I can forgive him." Billy is still quiet, but I sense his eyes searching for mine. I look up at him. "I won't."

"That's your choice."

"Choice?" My voice is scratchy with emotion. "There is no choice. It's just the way it is."

Billy's hands are on my shoulders. "There's always choice, Rosie. It's up to you to decide to forgive or not. I understand if you don't, but you need to own that decision."

I pull away. "You sound like my ex-therapist."

Billy doesn't respond.

I grab the extra napkins and blow my nose and wipe my face. I want to hold on to my anger because it has served a purpose all these years. It has protected me. But having my father admit his guilt by asking me to forgive him cracks something open in me. I feel vulnerable, and I want to close that hole as quickly as possible.

"Don't withdraw from me, Rosie."

I look at him again. "I'm sorry I never contacted you after

you saved me."

"I didn't save you."

"You did. You got me the hell out of here. It was a debt I could never repay, so I just kept running. You must have wondered what happened to me."

"I did. But I had to respect your instructions not to try to find you. When Andy told me you were here, I couldn't wait one second longer to see you."

"Even in a hurricane."

He nods. "Even in a hurricane."

"Can you forgive me?"

"I already did. Years ago."

"You're a bigger person than I am, Billy."

"I'm not. Well, I am physically, but size has nothing to do with the capacity to forgive or love. You're one of the bravest people I know. I believe that you could love someone and let them close if you just trusted yourself."

I look out at the harbor. Light sparkles off the water. The white reflections of the fishing boats glisten. What a difference a day makes. This harbor must have been all chop just yesterday during the hurricane. A large bird with slow wingbeats comes into view going south.

"Is that the roseate spoonbill?" I jump out of the truck.

Billy grabs small binoculars out of the glove compartment and rushes around to me. He looks at the bird. "Yes." He hands the glasses to me. "Mom always says spoonbills look like Jimmy Durante."

Although the bird isn't as tall as a great egret, which we have in abundance on Chincoteague and Assateague Islands, the roseate spoonbill looks longer in flight because of its big beak.

"I met some birders who braved the hurricane to come out to spot it," Billy says. "What a beauty. Glad I got to see it."

"She's going home after the storm."

We take turns watching the pink bird through the binoculars until it becomes a speck in the sky.

I put the glasses back in the truck. "You're right, you know, about me being able to love someone if I could trust myself, but I don't think I can take the chance."

"Have some faith."

"I don't know where to start."

He leans me against the truck and kisses me. Hormones I have controlled since the last time he kissed me rush alive. Amazed that I haven't forgotten how to do it, I kiss him back. His hands are in my hair. Every follicle responds with pure pleasure.

When we come up for air, I whisper, "Could I start with you?"

"I'd be honored." His eyes are burning with intensity. He runs his hands up and down my arms. "This is like a dream, Rosie. I can't believe you're here."

"You can't be any more surprised than I am. And what's more surprising is that I'm thinking about staying."

"Do you mean it? You'd really come back to The Tump?"

"Cross my heart." I run my fingers across my heart like we did as kids.

"I've been dying to ask you to stay, but it had to come from you if you were ready."

"I am ready, and I'm also ready to go out to Oyster Bay. It's time to put this thing to rest." I get back into the truck.

Billy returns to the driver's side and turns over the engine.

I feel years of heaviness melting off as the Chincoteague wind blows my hair around in the open cab. We stop at the light at Maddox and Main. The bridge out of here is to our left. Billy drove me over it to freedom twenty years ago. Ironically, I took my chains with me. The only way I'll free myself is to do it right here on this beautiful island, and I must deal with my father's ghost before I let Billy back into my life.

TIDEWATER WEDDING

C HELSEA TAPPED HER PENCIL on the kitchen table in the cozy Elizabeth Street apartment she and Bryan were renting in their hometown of Easton, Maryland. She glanced at her second trial wedding manicure. She had liked the first one fine, but her future mother-in-law had insisted she get another. Chelsea had to admit that her nails had never looked better, but it just wasn't that important to her.

"You've got to talk to your mother, Bryan." Chelsea drew a line through another name on their wedding guest list. "She's insisting on including your sister's sorority sisters on the guest list, which means I have to find more of my relatives and friends to cut."

Sitting across from her with his laptop, calculator, and several sketches and photographs spread around, Bryan sighed and added more figures to the landscape design estimate he was working on. "Wouldn't it be easier if we moved the wedding from the Crystal Room to the Gold Ballroom? Didn't the wedding planner say it held more people?"

Chelsea gripped her pencil. Her mother and Bryan's mother had selected the elegant Tidewater Inn for the wedding and reception. "For the sake of my father's health and sanity, we're trying to keep this a manageable size. This is the third wedding my parents are financing, and they made sure none of us had any college debt when we graduated."

"You'll be making plenty of money soon."

"Down the road, but since we decided not to wait to get married, Daddy is handling it." Chelsea double-checked the list. "As it is, we're inviting one hundred and twenty people. I know the Gold Ballroom holds twice that number, but it's too big and too expensive. We need to stick with the Crystal Room. I like it better anyway; it's lighter and brighter." She tried to calm her voice. "All of that's beside the point. I think it's unreasonable that your sister's wishes come before mine. Now, will you talk to your mother?"

"She won't listen to me." Bryan began jamming numbers into his calculator again. "I have to have this estimate in first thing tomorrow."

"Well, the wedding invitations have to go out."

"How many sorority sisters are we talking about? Not the entire house, I hope."

"Bryan, haven't you been listening to me? It doesn't matter if it's two or two hundred. The point is that I'm the bride, and my relatives matter more than your sister's sorority friends. When it's your sister's wedding, she can invite anyone she damn well pleases." Chelsea fought the tears she refused to show her fiancé.

"I understand how you feel, but why don't you ask your mom to talk to my mom? She may be able to make my mom see reason."

"You know that my mother always agrees with your mother." Chelsea got up to pour herself a glass of chardonnay. "How is it that your mother's and sister's wishes are more important to her than mine?"

"Listen, honey. Your mother loves you very much, but this history between our moms goes way back. I gave up fighting it years ago."

"If they were strangers, they wouldn't gang up on us like this."

"They do make an invincible team. Like I said, it's easier to just let them have their way."

"They've been having their way since we started dating in

high school." Chelsea gulped down some wine. "My senior prom gown and your tuxedo cummerbund had to be that awful pink because that's what they wanted. You hated that pink cummerbund. All the guys made jokes about it. Why didn't you stand up to your mother on that?" Chelsea plopped back down in her chair. "I even had to go to the University of Maryland because that's the college they wanted for both of us."

Bryan looked up from his work. "Hey, we wanted to go to the same college."

"I know, but your landscape architecture degree took priority over my finance degree."

"You can get a finance degree anywhere, and you did get the job you wanted."

"I wanted to get out of here." Chelsea stretched. "We needed some space, at least during college. It was the time to explore and try new things before we settled down."

"Yes!" Bryan mumbled to himself. "This estimate is coming in under budget."

Chelsea ran through the guest list again and tossed down the pencil. "I need you to talk to your mother. I refuse to cross off one more of my relatives or friends."

"Okay. I'll text her tomorrow." Bryan began typing on his laptop.

"No! Texting isn't going to do any good. You have to sit her down and tell her what's what, or I will." Chelsea stood, wine glass in hand.

"You'll what?" Bryan seemed to be getting more irritable.

"Nothing." Chelsea finished the rest of her wine. "I'm going to bed. To *sleep.*" She hoped that message was clear to Bryan.

"Chels, I'm sorry. I'll call her tomorrow after work."

"I'm still going to sleep." Chelsea put the glass in the dishwasher.

"Okay. I'll be in as soon as I tighten up this estimate."

Chelsea went back to their bedroom. She wanted to slam the door, but they lived on the second floor of a lovely duplex and she didn't want to disturb the neighbors. Chelsea liked that the house didn't look like apartments but blended in with other attractive homes similar to the one she hoped to own someday. Right now, she just wanted to forget everything. Then she remembered she hadn't set out her clothes for tomorrow's meeting. She had her first potential client coming in. If she landed this big fish, she'd feel she was proving herself to the firm that had hired her. It was her goal to establish herself as quickly as possible.

As Chelsea selected a blouse to go with the pale-blue suit that set off her eyes nicely, she realized how angry she was. Bryan was a wonderful guy. He had many great qualities, but he never stood up to his mom. It hadn't seemed like such a big deal until now. They were getting married, just as their mothers, who were best friends, had planned. Chelsea had thought it was better to wait a few years after graduating from college. They both needed to get their careers established. She could help pay for the wedding by then. But then Bryan had popped the question at their joint college graduation party. She couldn't remember if she was thrilled or shocked. Of course, she had said yes; being engaged didn't mean they had to rush into a wedding. But the mothers had had other ideas. The great wedding planning machine kicked in, and here they were, with the big date breathing down their necks.

After Chelsea set out the jewelry that best suited the colors she'd be wearing the next day, she went into the bathroom, removed her makeup, and washed her face. When she looked in the mirror, she didn't like how sad she looked. This was supposed to be the happiest time of her life, right? She dried her face and ran a brush through her light-brown hair. It was becoming clear to her that if they were to be married, Bryan had to put his wife before his mother. Chelsea wondered if that would ever happen, and if it didn't, whether she really wanted to marry him.

Bryan was the only man she'd ever been with, and she was not interested in dating strangers. Her skin crawled at the thought as she slipped on her long sleeping T-shirt and climbed into bed. It wasn't right to marry Bryan just because she didn't want to deal with the dating scene. She loved Bryan, but marrying him was beginning to mean too many compromises.

With celebration plans on her mind, Chelsea trotted from the office to her car after work. The attractive Easton Historic District with its brick buildings, antique stores, chic shops, and popular restaurants was bustling on this late afternoon. It was only a short drive across town to their apartment, and Chelsea would have a little time to relax and change before heading back into town with Bryan.

Chelsea had made dinner reservations at eight o'clock at Scossa. They weren't eating out often, as they were trying to live on the budget they had made in order to reach certain goals, but her client had signed, so she was feeling good. Bryan hadn't said anything about having talked to his mom, but he had let her know that his boss and the client were happy with his estimate. He thought they were going to get the design job. Under these circumstances, Chelsea felt they could splurge.

Just as she reached her car, a text came through from Karen, their wedding planner. "Please call me ASAP. We need to talk."

Chelsea texted back, "I'm in town. Should I just walk over?"

A moment later, she read, "Yes."

The two storefront windows of Karen's studio were filled with white wedding displays. As Chelsea entered the center door, she was surrounded with table settings, linens, flower arrangements, and everything bridal.

"Thanks for coming over." Karen shook her hand. "Let's go back to my office."

All their wedding planning had taken place out in the show-room, where samples and photographs were handy. Chelsea had never been back to Karen's office, which turned out to be a tiny section of the stockroom. Whatever she had to say was obviously serious enough for Karen to take her where they wouldn't be disturbed.

Chelsea's heart began to race at she sat in the chair across from Karen's desk. "Has something fallen through?"

"Nothing like that." Karen pushed a lock of blonde hair behind her ear. "Honestly, I've never run into quite this situation, and I hope I'm doing the right thing."

"Please, just tell me."

"Your mother and Bryan's mother came in a little while ago."

Chelsea sensed something bad had happened, but she couldn't imagine what. They had made all their decisions weeks ago, so why on earth would the mothers be in here talking to Karen? "Go on."

"They ordered a chocolate fountain for the wedding reception."

"I can't believe it." Chelsea took a breath. "Actually, I can. Those two are out of hand."

"I reminded them that you and Bryan had expressly said you didn't want one."

Chelsea shifted in the chair. "I don't have anything against chocolate fountains in the right setting. I agreed to have one for the bridal shower. I mean, women do love anything dipped in chocolate, but I wanted to keep things elegant for the reception."

"I totally agree." Karen fiddled with a pen. "There's more."

"Go on."

"On their way out the door, I heard Mrs. Cleveland say to your mother, 'That will teach Bryan to interfere with my guest list.'"

So, Bryan must have confronted his mother. Chelsea felt a tiny bit of hope bubble up in her chest. Still, she couldn't help but mutter, "*Her* guest list? Is she the bride?"

"Exactly!" Karen put the pen back down. "I don't like to meddle in family business, but *you* are the bride."

Chelsea got up. "Can I give you a hug?"

Karen rose and came around her desk. "Of course."

"You did the right thing," Chelsea said as she wrapped her arms around Karen. "I'll make sure the mothers don't know that you gave me a heads-up." Chelsea headed toward the door. "I can say I came by to talk about something else, and you innocently said, 'So you changed your mind about a chocolate fountain.'"

Karen's worried face relaxed. "Thanks."

Chelsea dashed back to her car. She knew that one negative review from a well-respected matron like her mother or her future mother-in-law could hurt a business like Karen's. The entire drive home, Chelsea seethed. *This has got to stop.* She pulled into her parking spot behind the duplex. Bryan's vehicle was there, too.

"I'm home," Chelsea called out as she put her briefcase away. Getting no response, she went into the bedroom. "Bryan?"

She heard "Just getting out of the shower" from behind the half-open bathroom door, so she stuck her head in.

"I'm home."

Bryan opened the shower door and grabbed a towel. "Hi, honey."

Chelsea felt herself weaken. They had been intimate since they were in high school, but he still overwhelmed her sense of control.

She watched his muscles flex as he toweled off. "We have to talk."

"What did I do now?" He pouted a little and then laughed. When he reached up to dry his dark-blond hair, a few drops of water still clung to his chest and tight abdomen. She didn't dare look down.

"I'll be in the kitchen getting something to drink." Chelsea skirted out the door. She couldn't let him seduce her, not now. Then she remembered the meddling mothers and was so angry, she thought she could knock down one of the Ravens' linebackers.

She'd drunk most of her ginger ale by the time Bryan came in wearing khakis and a short-sleeved shirt. "If you're staying in your suit, I'm not dressed enough." His hair was still damp. He'd not bothered to use the hair dryer.

"I'll change in a minute, but I don't know if we're going."

"Couldn't you get a reservation?"

"Yes. It's for eight o'clock."

"What's the problem?"

Although she didn't think she could stay still, Chelsea sat at the table. "Please sit down."

"You're freaking me out, Chels." Bryan pulled out a chair.

"You talked to your mom?"

"Yes, she was ridiculous, but we agreed that she would only invite five of the sorority sisters."

"Five? That means I still have to cut five from my side."

"Please be reasonable, Chelsea. It was the best I could negotiate."

"You didn't negotiate anything. She gets to invite five sorority sisters, and she gets a chocolate fountain."

"What?"

"Karen contacted me as I was leaving work. Our mothers were in her studio, adding a chocolate fricking fountain as retribution for you asking her to drop the sorority girls."

"Well, a chocolate fountain isn't that bad. Lots of people like them." Bryan reached across the table for her hand.

"Don't touch me right now."

Bryan stood up. "I've had enough unreasonable female family members for one day."

"You're putting me in the same category as your mother?" Chelsea pushed her chair back and rose. The table separated them.

"Look, if you want to get to dinner on time, you'd better change."

"I'm not going." Chelsea sat back down and smoothed over the placemat with her hands in an effort to calm herself, but she felt on the edge of tears.

"Chels, you just have to relax. It's one day. Let the mothers do their thing. It's still going to be wonderful."

"If we don't put a stop to their meddling, it will never end. They'll be picking names for our children and telling us how to raise them."

"That's what mothers do."

"No. They don't. They back off and allow their children to live their own lives. They give advice when it is requested. Your mother went behind our backs and purposely ordered something we didn't want for our wedding reception."

"She probably forgot we didn't want one."

"No, Bryan. She didn't forget anything. Karen overheard your mom say that adding the chocolate fountain would teach us a lesson for meddling with her guest list. It was intentional. Doesn't that piss you off?"

Bryan shrugged and sat down. "I guess so, but your mother was a part of it."

"I know she was. However, I don't think she'd get so involved if your mother weren't egging her on."

"There's nothing we can do about it."

Chelsea felt like she was carrying the weight of the world, and there was no more energy to hold in her tears.

"Oh, darling. Please don't cry."

"Bryan, I don't want to get married."

He was stunned into silence.

"I'm crying because it hurts so much to say this to you, but I can't marry someone who isn't willing to fight for me. Fight for himself, really. I can handle my own battles, but you let your mother bully you.

"But—"

"You do whatever she wants. It's time to grow up." Chelsea stood. "I'm calling off the wedding. I'll move out as soon as I find someplace to go. I'm sorry to hurt you. I love you, but I'm not happy." Chelsea strode into the bedroom and shut the door. She texted the restaurant to cancel her celebratory dinner and cried herself to sleep.

Chelsea woke up when she heard voices in the apartment. They were loud and growing louder. She couldn't imagine what was going on. Had Bryan gone crazy and invited friends over for a party? Was he that glad to get out of marrying her? She stormed out of the bedroom. She must have had a wild look on her face because her parents, Bryan's parents, Bryan's sister, and their wedding planner, Karen, fell quiet at her appearance.

"What's going on, Bryan?" Chelsea asked, staring at the assembled group.

"What's going on," Mrs. Cleveland interrupted, "is my son has become rude to his mother."

"No, Mom, I haven't. It's time that Chelsea comes first in my life. I'm sorry if that hurts you. You are still a major priority." Bryan looked at his dad sitting in the easy chair. "You are, too, Pops, but things have to change. *I* have to change."

Chelsea wasn't sure she had heard Bryan correctly, but from the look on his mother's face, she had a feeling that she had.

"I told all of you to come over here because we're canceling the wedding unless everyone in this room agrees to our terms. Bryan looked at her beseechingly. "I love you, Chelsea. I haven't been putting you first, and if you still don't want to marry me, I'll understand. But I want to try to set things straight."

"Well, I'll tell you what's going to be set straight around here." Bryan's mother glared at Karen. "You're not going to book another Easton wedding, if I have anything to say about it."

Karen was about the only person Chelsea had any sympathy for at this point. "Karen had nothing to do with it. I went over there to see about trying to squeeze in five sorority sisters, and Karen innocently mentioned that she was glad I had changed my mind about the chocolate fountain."

Bryan's sister, who was sprawled on the floor, looked up from her phone. "I don't care about inviting my sorority sisters. They'd just be bored to death, anyway." She went back to texting.

Karen looked at Chelsea from across the room. "Thanks for trying to cover for me, but I already told them that I alerted you to the change." She shifted to make sure Mrs. Cleveland could see her clearly from her perch against a windowsill. "The bride comes first in my business. It's even my new marketing platform. 'Putting the BRIDE back in bridal planning.'"

Chelsea's mom blurted out from the sofa, "I'm sure many young women would appreciate that." Then she sheepishly looked to her best friend.

"Mom, why do you do that? Why can't you speak your mind around Bryan's mother? When my older sisters made decisions, you never ran to anyone else for advice. You didn't interfere with their weddings. You put them first. Why is it different with me?"

Chelsea's father said to his wife, "Ellen, don't you think it's time you stood up for yourself?"

"What exactly is he talking about?" Bryan's mom asked. "Stood up to me?"

"Yes, that's what he means." Chelsea's mom cleared her throat. "I've always felt unworthy of you, Marian."

"Well, that's just ridiculous."

"I need you to stay quiet for one damn minute, Marian." Chelsea's mom rose to her feet. "You were the cool girl, the popular girl. I cared so much about being your friend that I was willing to do just about anything to keep you from dumping me. I got so used to agreeing with everything you said, I lost track of my own opinion."

"If you lost track of your own opinion, that's on you," Mrs. Cleveland said.

Chelsea's mom glanced down only briefly before taking a step toward her friend. "You're right. You wanted to be in control, so I let you."

"Well, someone has to get things done. If I waited for you to make a decision, we'd never accomplish anything."

"Not exactly, Marian. I did make decisions and have opinions; you just always ignored them or ran right over them."

Mrs. Cleveland opened her mouth to speak.

"No, I'm not finished. I allowed you to take charge, and that's fine if I'm the only one compromising. It's different now because it's affecting our children."

Bryan's mother appeared to be taking all of this in.

"I care about you deeply, Marian. You're my dearest friend. I don't want to hurt you, but I think this pattern has to stop when it comes to my daughter's happiness . . . and your son's happiness, too."

Chelsea noticed her mom's hands were trembling, which wasn't a surprise; however, Bryan's mother's face softened in a way that Chelsea had never seen before.

"Mom?" Bryan looked concerned.

Bryan's mom's shoulders trembled, and she sniffed. His dad handed her his handkerchief and patted her back. When she composed herself, she slipped over to sit next to Chelsea's mom. "Ellen, forgive me. You're right. I never realized the sacrifices you were making to stay in my good graces. After a while, I just assumed you agreed with me on everything. We were a team, but you were actually putting me before your own daughter. I'm sorry." She focused on Chelsea, who felt like she was in a dream. "I hope you can forgive me, Chelsea. And Bryan. No chocolate fountain, no extra guests from my side, and, Karen, put the cake top back to what they wanted originally."

Karen gasped. "I'd forgotten about that."

Everyone giggled nervously. The tension in the room began to dissipate, but there was still one thing keeping everyone on edge.

Bryan knelt on one knee in front of Chelsea. "Chelsea, will you still marry me? I love you beyond anything I can comprehend. I don't want my life without you in it. We can elope, we can postpone, we can get married in a damn chocolate fountain for all I care. I'll do whatever will make you happy."

Bryan's affirmation brought tears to Chelsea's eyes. "Yes. Yes! You're the only man I've ever wanted. Of course I'll still marry you." She threw her arms around his neck and kissed him with all her might.

Their small apartment was filled with cheers. Even Bryan's sister put down her phone and clapped.

With less than an hour before the garden ceremony, Chelsea and her bridesmaids worked on final touches in their Tidewater Inn suite. While everyone else was distracted by helping Bryan's sister decide which color lipstick to wear, Chelsea said to her maid of honor, "I'm so glad to hear your dad is recovering from his stroke."

Kaleigh smiled. "He's getting better every day."

"And I'm glad you brought Evan to the rehearsal dinner last night. He's nice, and you two have so much in common. He builds boats, and now you're running your dad's boat."

"He and Bryan seemed to get along." Kaleigh touched up Chelsea's hair.

"Bryan likes him. He told me that Evan invited us out to his cottage with you after our honeymoon."

Kaleigh held up a hand mirror. "Check the back now. You look beautiful."

"Thanks. So do you, and from what I've observed, Evan thinks you're hot."

Kaleigh blushed. "I like him, but I'm taking it real slow after Dirk the Jerk."

"Nothing wrong with that."

Chelsea's mom arrived wearing a turquoise dress. She carried a small gift box.

"Mom, you look fabulous!" Chelsea and her sisters fussed for a moment over their mother.

"Ladies, do you mind if I have a few minutes alone with my daughter?"

The room was vacated with the sound of swishing formal gowns.

"Mom, I'm so nervous." Chelsea sat at an antique vanity looking in the mirror.

"You still don't have your gown on. Are you having second thoughts?"

"No. Uncle Phillip created a one-of-a-kind masterpiece for me. I just don't want it mussed."

"My brother was always better at sewing than me. It drove

your grandmother crazy until Phillip took her to New York to see the first show he costumed. He is a genius, and he's outdone himself on your gown. It is stunning."

"Maybe you can help me put it on at the very last minute?"

"It would be an honor." Her mom pulled a Chippendale chair over next to Chelsea and sat. "Now what are you nervous about?"

"I feel so isolated up here with the girls. It's kind of weird. How are things downstairs?"

"Everyone is ready and waiting for you."

"How's Bryan? He hasn't run away, has he?"

Her mom chuckled. "No. He's pacing around like an expectant father."

"Slow down, Mom! We'll get to that eventually."

"I can wait."

"Any surprises with the guests? Who did Uncle Phillip bring?"

"His friend Kate, who just completed a highly acclaimed run as Mrs. Lovett in *Sweeney Todd* at the Garfield Center. She's now the toast of Chestertown."

"How cool. Didn't she get divorced?"

"Yes, but Phillip is helping her relaunch her life and apparently her acting career." Chelsea's mom sighed. "I wish he'd meet a good man."

"I wish Aunt Devyn would meet someone, too. Hey, what about that friend of Dad's who moved back from California. You know, the one who's a vineyard consultant."

"Sam Woodrich?"

"That's the one. Oh, but he may be a little too old for Aunt Devyn."

"He's already off the market."

"That was fast."

"He's dating Kate's sister."

"The one who's a barber in Cambridge?"

"Yes. Trudy. Apparently they knew one another in high school."

"Well, the high school romance worked for Bryan and me." Chelsea paused. "Maybe Aunt Devyn should go to a class reunion."

"No need. She has met someone."

Chelsea squealed with delight. "Tell me."

"Your father's sister is dating a new professor from Salisbury University. He's with her today. He just moved back to the Eastern Shore after years in Manhattan. Devyn helped him find a dog, and one thing led to another. He's handsome, smart, a great father to his two kids. And Jason likes him."

"You are full of surprises and good news."

Her mother's eyes sparkled. "I do have one more surprise. Your cousin Billy is here from Chincoteague with a woman he's been in love with since childhood, and she remembers you as a toddler from the summers we spent vacationing with my sister's family."

"Really?" Chelsea thought back. "Was her name Rosie?"

"Yes. Well, it's Becca Rose, but since Billy called her Rosie, we all did. She spent a lot of time at my sister's because her father was cruel to her. You were only about five when she left Chincoteague. How could you remember her?"

"I remember that she seemed sad, but she was always nice to me."

Chelsea's mom looked at her watch. "Oh, it's nearly time."

Chelsea shuddered. "I'm so nervous. I just want everything to be perfect. God, how did women used to get married without having sex first? I can't imagine that kind of pressure on top of all this."

"I don't know."

"Wow! So you and Daddy?"

"Well, I guess the jig is up."

"I love it! You're normal."

Her mother smirked. "I don't know how normal I am, but I was and still am very attracted to your father."

"Yeah, he's still pretty cute." Chelsea winked. "For an old guy who's my dad."

"Who are you calling 'old'?"

They laughed together.

"Mom, I feel like we're becoming more than daughter and mother. We're becoming friends. I like that."

"I do, too. I have something for you, Chels."

"You've done too much already."

"A mother can never do too much for her daughter." She presented Chelsea with a wrapped box.

Chelsea untied the ribbon and found inside a lace handkerchief.

"Something borrowed. It was your grandmother's. I carried it for my wedding. My mother told me then that if I followed my heart, I would always be happy. She knew I was doing that when I chose your father."

"Oh, Mom. That's wonderful. It's so special that it was Nanna's and you carried it. At first I thought maybe it was one of the antique hankies you bought in Berlin as bridal shower gifts. You know, they were a big hit."

"Not as big as the chocolate fountain." Her mother's eyes wrinkled with humor.

"Oh, the eff-ing chocolate fountain."

"Chels, if we're friends, you can go ahead and curse in front of me."

"No way. I could never say that word in front of you."

"Still your mama."

Chelsea threw her arms around her mother. "Always."

Tilghman Island Country Store Potato Salad
Miss Peggy's Special Recipe

Ingredients

4 pounds potatoes, peeled and cubed
1/2 teaspoon salt
1/2 large yellow onion, peeled, minced in small pieces
1/2 tablespoon celery seed
Black pepper, to taste
2 cups sugar
1/8 cup apple cider vinegar
1/2 tablespoon mustard
2 cups mayonnaise

Directions

1. Cover potatoes with water and bring to a boil.
2. Add salt to water and cook potatoes until tender.
3. Drain potatoes in colander.
4. When potatoes have cooled, add celery seed, onion, and black pepper. Mix well into cooled potatoes.
5. In a separate bowl, mix sugar and vinegar until dissolved.
6. Add mustard and mix well.
7. Add mayonnaise and mix well.
8. Add mayonnaise mixture to potatoes and mix well. Adjust salt and pepper to taste.

Delicious warm or cold

Audrey's Peaches and Cream Pie

Courtesy of Barbara Osborne

Ingredients

1 9-inch unbaked deep-dish pie crust
6-8 peaches, peeled and halved (or sliced)
2/3 cup sugar
4 tablespoons flour
1/4 teaspoon salt
1/2 teaspoon cinnamon
1 cup half-and-half or light cream

Directions

1. Preheat oven to 350 degrees.
2. Place pie crust in ovenproof pie pan.
3. Arrange peach halves, flat side down, in the prepared pie crust.
4. Mix sugar, flour, salt, and cinnamon in a bowl.
5. Add the half-and-half or light cream to the dry ingredients. Mix well.
6. Pour the creamy mix over the peaches in the crust.
7. Bake at 350 degrees for 40-45 minutes or until cream mixture has solidified and crust is golden brown.
8. Cool before serving.

Devyn's Three-Bean Salad

Courtesy of Mickey Allen

Ingredients

2 cans red kidney beans
1 can garbanzo beans
1 can cannellini beans
1 head garlic
Olive oil
Red wine vinegar

Directions

1. Drain and wash beans thoroughly in a colander. Place beans in a container that has a lid.
2. Chop one full head of garlic and add to beans.
3. Add enough olive oil to reach one inch below the top of the beans.
4. Add enough red wine vinegar to just cover the beans.
5. Store in refrigerator. Keep the beans covered in the vinegar and oil.

Sam's Peanut Butter Chocolate Cocomacs
Courtesy of Gary Collings

Ingredients

2 cups flour
1 teaspoon baking soda
1 teaspoon salt
1 cup butter, softened
1/4 cup granulated sugar
1/4 cup light brown sugar, packed
1 cup dark brown sugar, packed
2 large eggs
2 1/2 teaspoons vanilla extract
3/4 cup macadamia nuts, coarsely chopped
10-12 ounces peanut butter chips
10-12 ounces semi-sweet chocolate chips
1 1/3 cups sweetened flaked coconut, plus extra for optional topping

Directions

1. In a bowl, stir together flour, baking soda, and salt.
2. In a separate bowl, beat the sugars and butter using an electric hand mixer until well mixed.

3. Beat in the eggs and vanilla.

4. Beat in the flour mixture and continue beating until no white streaks remain.

5. Stir in both kinds of chips, macadamia nuts, and coconut until combined.

6. Cover dough with plastic wrap and chill for at least two hours in refrigerator.

7. Preheat oven to 350 degrees.

8. Line cookie sheets with parchment paper.

9. Form cookie dough into 1 1/4-inch balls.

10. Drop dough onto the cookie sheets about 2 inches apart.

11. Gently push a pinch of extra coconut onto the top of each cookie ball before baking (optional).

12. Bake 10-12 minutes or until the edges just begin to brown.

13. Allow to cool on the pan for 3 minutes before removing to cooling rack to cool completely.

14. Store leftover cookies in a covered container.

Eastern Shore Crab Cakes

Ingredients

1 egg

4-5 tablespoons mayonnaise

3 teaspoons Dijon mustard

1 tablespoon lemon juice

1 cup unsalted saltines or other low-salt cracker, ground in blender to crumbs

1/8 cup chopped scallions or red onion

3 teaspoons (or to taste) Old Bay seafood seasoning

1-2 tablespoons fresh parsley

1 pound Eastern Shore crab meat

Oil for pan frying

Directions

1. Whisk egg, mayonnaise, mustard, and lemon juice.
2. Mix in cracker crumbs, onion, seasoning mix, and parsley.
3. Gently fold in crab meat.
4. Mold into patties.
5. Refrigerate at least 1 hour.
6. Heat oil in skillet and pan fry until crusty on the outside and cooked through on the inside.

Chef Copper's Snapping Turtle Soup
Courtesy of The Tidewater Inn

Soup Ingredients

1 snapping turtle (12-14 pounds), cleaned
1 gallon prepared turtle stock, homemade or commercial
1 gallon water
27 ounces tomatoes
54 ounces tomato puree
1 tablespoon lemon juice
1 tablespoon Tabasco
1 teaspoon Worcestershire sauce
1 bay leaf
1/2 teaspoon pickling spice
1/2 teaspoon salt
A pinch of pepper
2 stalks of celery, chopped
1 onion, chopped
1 pound cooked beef bones
2 pounds chicken or turkey carcasses

Roux Ingredients

1/2 cup butter
1/2 cup flour

Directions

1. Combine soup ingredients in a large stockpot.
2. Simmer until the meat is tender.
3. Remove the turtle from the pot, strip the carcass of meat, and then dice the meat. Set aside.
4. Strain the stock.
5. Make the roux by melting the butter in a skillet over low heat, gradually sprinkling in the flour and stirring until the mixture is browned.
6. Add the roux and diced turtle meat to the strained stock.

Serve with sherry, if desired.

Eastern Shore Shorts Road Trip

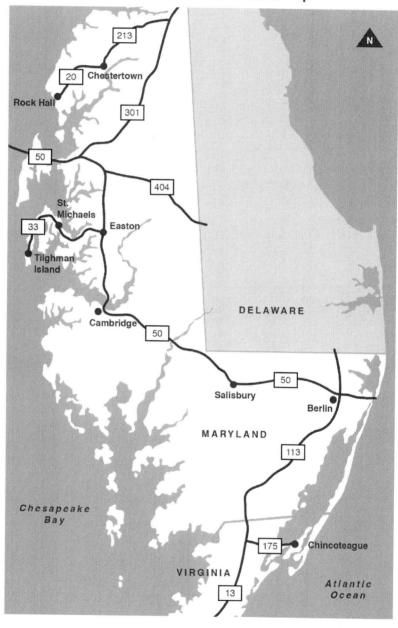

Road Trip Index of Towns from *Eastern Shore Shorts* (North to South)

Chestertown, Maryland, the setting for "Drama Queen"

Founded in 1706 and home to Washington College, The Garfield Center for the Arts at the Prince Theatre, Kent County Arts Council, and Sultana Projects. Strong arts and theatre community, wonderful shops and galleries. Popular events include First Fridays, Sultana Downrigging, Chestertown Tea Party Festival, Harry Potter Festival, Chestertown Jazz Festival, and Farmers' Market.

Rock Hall, Maryland, the setting for "Waterwoman"

Known as the Pearl of the Chesapeake, this harbor village is on the Chesapeake Bay and is home to many watermen and the Watermen's Museum and the Eastern Neck National Wildlife Refuge. Popular events include Rockfish Tournament, Watermen's Day, Pirates and Wenches Fantasy Weekend, and Fall Fest in Rock Hall. Check out The Mainstay for great live music and cultural events.

St. Michaels and Tilghman Island, Maryland, the settings for "The Cottage"

Along with being the home of the Chesapeake Bay Maritime Museum, St. Michaels has many great shops, galleries, and restaurants. Popular events include the Annual East Coast Decoy Collectors Buy, Swap, and Sell, Eastern Shore Sea Glass and Coastal Arts Festival, Annual Antique and Classic Boat Festival, and Mid-Atlantic Small Crafts Festival. Tilghman Island is a small island (less than three miles long and a mile wide) at the end of the Bay Hundred peninsula. The first English settlers arrived in 1656. Kayak, sail, and fish in this beautiful setting, and be sure to check out the Tilghman Island Country Store, Phillips Wharf Environmental Center, and Tilghman Island Watermen's Museum.

Easton, Maryland, the setting for "Tidewater Wedding"

Easton is the Talbot County Seat with a handsome brick courthouse and a statue of Abolitionist Frederick Douglass on the lawn. Beautiful downtown area with shops, galleries, and restaurants. Popular events include Annual Waterfowl Festival, the Chesapeake Film Festival, and Chesapeake Chamber Music Festival. Check out what's going on at the Avalon Theatre, Talbot Historical Society Museum and Garden, Academy Art Museum, and the Easton Farmers Market.

Cambridge, Maryland, the setting for "Crab Cake Tango" and "Leaps of Faith"

Cambridge is one of the oldest colonial towns in Maryland. In 1684, the English settled where the Choptank Indians lived along the Choptank River. Cambridge became a seaport community and has a rich maritime heritage. Home of the Dorchester Center for the Arts, Sailwinds Park, and Choptank River Lighthouse. Popular events include Second Saturdays, Annual Crawfish Boil and Muskrat Stew Fest, Taste of Cambridge Crab Cook-Off and Free Street Festival, and GrooveFEST: Blues, Brews, and BBQs. Be sure to check out the nearby Harriet Tubman Underground Railroad Visitor Center and Blackwater National Wildlife Refuge.

Salisbury, Maryland, the setting for "Peacemaker Puppy"

Home of Salisbury University, Salisbury Zoo, Ward Museum of Waterfowl Art, and Pemberton Historical Park. Salisbury will host the National Folk Festival 2018-2022. Be sure to check out Third Fridays.

Berlin, Maryland, the setting for "Antiques"

Voted America's Coolest Town 2014, Berlin was the location for two major films: *Runaway Bride* and *Tuck Everlasting*. Home of many great antique shops, stores, galleries, and Salt Water Media. Popular events include Second Fridays, Annual Bathtub Races, Spring and Fall Cruisers, and Jazz and Blues Bash.

Chincoteague, Virginia, the setting for "Homeward Migration"

Chincoteague is said to be an Indian name for "beautiful land across the water." Chincoteague National Wildlife Refuge and Assateague Island National Seashore are hotspots for birding, swimming, fishing, boating, hiking, and seeing wild ponies. Check out the Museum of Chincoteague, the Captain Timothy Hill House, Sundial Books, and the Assateague Lighthouse. Many places to lodge, eat, and shop. Make reservations in advance if staying for the Annual Pony Swim.

ERICK SAHLER
ORIGINAL HAND-PULLED
SERIGRAPHS

You won't find any geese or skipjacks in the
limited-edition silkscreen prints of Erick Sahler.

His "Eastern Shore art for the rest of us" ™
salutes some of the more esoteric charms of life
on Delmarva, including Smith Island cake,
the Delmar stock car races and
the old Chincoteague swing bridge.

Hand-pulled one color at a time in his Salisbury, Md.,
studio, all Sahler's limited-edition serigraphs
are unique works of pop art.

You can find them in shops across Delmarva.
For a list of his sellers, to order a piece online
or for more information, visit www.ErickSahler.com
or call 410-845-3774.

"Eastern Shore art for the rest of us" ™

www.ErickSahler.com

If you enjoyed *Eastern Shore Shorts*

Sandy Shorts

What do you get when you combine bad dogs, bad men, and bad luck? Great beach reads. From sunny days of fun, through shifting sands of change and stormy skies of conflict, to starry nights of romance, this collection of short stories is the perfect addition to your beach bag. You'll smile with recognition as characters in the stories ride the Cape May-Lewes Ferry, barhop in Dewey, stroll through Bethany Beach, and run into the waves in Rehoboth.

The Sea Sprite Inn

Jillian has lived through more than her share of tough times, but leaps at a chance to reinvent herself when she inherits a dilapidated family beach house. Now, along with bath towels and restaurant recommendations, she offers advice, insights, and encouragement—with a side dish of humor— as owner of The Sea Sprite Inn in Rehoboth. As guests come and go, each with unique challenges and discoveries, Jillian learns to trust her instincts and finds a clear path to her future.

Rehoboth Beach Reads Series

These anthologies are jam-packed with just the sorts of stories you love to read at the beach. Each contains 20-25 delightful tales from a variety of genres, authored by many different talented writers.

Beach Love

From a romance novelist who longs for a love of her own to a woman who finds love in another era, and from a love-struck wrestler to a real-life Cinderella, the characters in these stories head to the beach to find that perfect someone.

www.catandmousepress.com

Gail Priest is the author of the Annie Crow Knoll series, which is comprised of three books: *Annie Crow Knoll: Sunrise* debuted in 2013, *Annie Crow Knoll: Sunset* was released in 2014, and *Annie Crow Knoll: Moonrise* was published in 2016. She was honored to have an excerpt from *Sunset* chosen for PS Publishing's anthology, *Fifty Women Over Fifty*.

A native of Collingswood, NJ, Gail now lives in Haddon Heights, NJ. For seventeen years, she and her husband rented a cottage in Betterton, MD, on the Chesapeake Bay in a cottage community that was the inspiration for the Annie Crow Knoll trilogy and led to the publication of *Eastern Shore Shorts*.

Gail is also a playwright. Her play *Eva's Piano* was produced at the Dayton Playhouse in their New Play Festival. The Church Hill Theatre in Church Hill, MD, staged a reading of her play *A Thing with Feathers*.

Following the release of *Eastern Shore Shorts*, Gail will be working on a novel with a paranormal twist.

Visit Gail's website: http://gailpriest.com

Facebook: www.facebook.com/AuthorGailPriest

Newsletter: Tiny.cc/nueatx

Other Books by Gail Priest

Made in the USA
Middletown, DE
18 February 2022

61453334R00125